*first*

*comes*

*love*

BY **KATIE KACVINSKY**

Houghton Mifflin
HOUGHTON MIFFLIN HARCOURT
BOSTON   NEW YORK   2012

Houghton Mifflin is an imprint of Houghton Mifflin Harcourt Publishing Company.

www.hmhbooks.com

The text of this book is set in Aldus LT Std.

Library of Congress Cataloging-in-Publication Data
Kacvinsky, Katie.
First comes love / by Katie Kacvinsky.
p. cm.
Summary: Ten months after his twin sister dies, with his family falling apart,
Gray Thomas meets an unusual girl at the community college who makes
him think life is interesting again.
ISBN 978-0-547-59979-3
[1. Love—Fiction. 2. Death—Fiction. 3. Family problems—Fiction.
4. Twins—Fiction. 5. Sisters—Fiction.] I. Title.
PZ7.K116457Fir 2012
[Fic]—dc22
2011006266

Manufactured in the United States of America
DOC 10 9 8 7 6 5 4 3 2 1
4500349134

## To Becky

*Thanks for sharing so much.*
*I'm sorry I never had the privilege*
*of knowing Dan.*

# ⏐⏐⏐ First Meet ⏐⏐⏐

## Gray

*Out of the corner of my eye, I'm watching a girl.* She's on the opposite side of the courtyard from me. The sun is pounding down on her bare shoulders. Her face is pressed up against a camera, and she's squatting low to the ground. It looks like an old manual camera by the way she focuses the lens and turns a lever after every shot.

The courtyard between us is really just ample cement sidewalks converging in a circular cement center. Apparently, whoever designed the landscape of Mesa Community College, felt this cheap material would suffice for students who are here on a budget and don't deserve a luxury landscape. Ivy League schools get Corinthian columns, cobblestone promenades, and brick halls surrounded by gardens so students can read Ernest Hemingway next to granite fountains and quote Robert Frost in terraces covered with climbing vines. Community college students get cement benches and a lone cafeteria specializing in greasy doughnuts and potato wedges. It puts us in our place from day one.

My eyes are drawn back to this strange girl. You can't help but notice her — she's always roaming around outside, like she's part coyote. Sometimes she sits against a tree and writes in a notebook no bigger than the palm of her hand. Sometimes she draws on a sketchpad. Sometimes she whistles. She's always by herself. She wears the same beat-up black Adidas tennis shoes every day. I think I used to own the same pair, when I was twelve.

She wears baggy jeans, an interesting style choice since the average summer temperature in Phoenix is a hundred and ten degrees. The jeans practically slide off her bony hips, and the bottoms flap like bird's wings in the dusty wind gusts. Today her tank top is the color of the sun, a citrus yellow, and it's too small, hugging her long, slender waist. She has the curves of a beanpole. Once she caught me watching her and grinned, but I immediately looked away. I don't want to acknowledge her. I'm not looking to make friends. I just want a diversion, an object to rest my eyes on so I can zone out and wait for time to pass.

I lean against a wall of the science building, which offers a sliver of shade, and pull my baseball cap low over my forehead to block out the bright light reflecting off the pavement. I always wear a hat to class. I feel like I can hide behind it, like I have the power to shun the world simply by lowering its rim. I pretend people can't see me and I can stare at whoever I want, mostly girls, in their skirts that fall barely below their hips, in high heels that show off their tan legs, and skintight tank tops that leave little to the imagination, which is fine with me.

I pick up my iPod and scroll through the albums until I find rap. I think music is seasonal. In the summer my taste changes. More hip hop, upbeat, fast-paced. In the winter it slows down. More acoustic and oldies. I drum my fingers against the ground and delay going to class until the last possible second. There is nothing more painful than taking math and creative writing in the middle of the summer. It's too much forced right and left brain activity to be asked of a person before noon. At least the misery comes in a concentrated dose of four weeks and not an entire semester.

My eyes wander back to this girl—now lying flat on her stomach in the middle of the sidewalk. I can feel myself glaring at her. What is she doing? Taking pictures of the stupid concrete? I watch her, baffled, and scan her lanky body. She isn't skinny like models in magazines—emaciated skinny, people who look like stick figures with big hair and makeup. She looks hyper skinny, as if she can't sit still long enough to eat a full meal. As if her secret diet is living life at a vivacious speed.

I check the time on my phone and look back at her with a frown. Of course she has to be monopolizing the one path between me and the English building. I could walk around her, but I've never seen someone photographing a sidewalk with such dedication, and I'm curious to know what's luring her to put her face inches from the ground. I stand up and take cautious steps toward her like I'm approaching a wild animal that could thrash out unexpectedly. She's sprawled out, her chest supported by her bony elbows, her hands holding the camera perfectly still. She must have heard me coming.

"Don't walk any closer," she warns. I stop a few feet away, and the wind picks up sand around us. Wisps of brown hair fall free from her braid and blow in her face. I frown at her for hogging a public walkway.

"You're blocking the sidewalk," I say. My throat's dry and my voice comes out raw and scratchy. She slowly turns her neck to face me and her eyes are intense on mine, serious in her mission.

"You'll scare them away," she whispers, and motions with her eyes. I look down at the empty path. There isn't a single movement in the distance. I stare back at her with concern. Maybe she's schizophrenic. Maybe the desert heat has fried her brain (at least the logical side) and she's hallucinating. I lift my foot to back up, but then I glance down and realize only a few inches away from this girl's head are two pale green geckos. They're facing each other as if they're talking.

I keep still and watch her turn the camera lens with delicate precision. She presses a button and I hear a subtle click.

"Got it," she says. She stands up and brushes the sand off her jeans. She's taller than I thought, only a few inches shorter than I am, and I'm six foot three.

"It's hard to get those buggers to sit still," she says. She smiles and her light brown eyes meet mine. "Definitely camera-shy."

I study her. She must be from out of town. My guess is the Midwest or out east.

"You're not from around here, are you?" I look at her skin, covered in freckles but paler than native Arizonians', who acquire enough daily sun to give their melanin a year-round stain of tan.

"What makes you say that?" she asks, and squints up at me.

Because you're acting nuts.

"You don't see many locals sacrificing their bodies on hot cement to get a close-up shot of geckos," I tell her. "They're everywhere."

She looks at the ground for more lizards. "They're so friendly. They always play tag around my feet." She places a black cap over the camera lens. "I'm visiting for the summer," she says, in answer to my question. I raise my eyebrows. Normally I'd be gone at this point. Small talk isn't my thing. But this girl is becoming more bizarre by the minute.

"You moved to Phoenix for the *summer?*" I ask, and she smiles at my shock. Most people flee the desert this time of year, unless you like feeling your skin bake or you enjoy spending your days inside a cool refrigerator commonly referred to as air conditioning.

"I've always wanted to see the desert," she says, and raises her chin. "What are you doing after class?" My mouth drops open at her assertiveness. Does she actually think I walked over to talk to her? Doesn't she realize she was just blocking my way?

"Uhm," I stammer. My daily routine is the same: eat lunch, play video games, strum my guitar, lift weights, try to figure out my life. Stay out of my parents' way. Work part-time at Video Hutch.

"Could you give me a ride home?" she asks.

I stall and pretend to check something on my phone while I think of an excuse.

"I rode the bus over from Scottsdale, and it took two hours to get here," she adds.

My mouth drops open with shock *again*. Who moves to Phoenix without a car? A weird jean-wearing, ride-mooching girl, that's who.

"You live in Phoenix without a car?"

"No, I have one," she tells me. "I just prefer riding the bus. I can see more of the city that way. But today you can be my tour guide."

I frown at her for presuming I have nothing better to do this afternoon than drag her around town. I mean, it's true, but it's rude of her to assume it. Besides, any normal person wouldn't be this forward with a stranger. And who actually enjoys riding a city bus? It's like a ghetto on wheels.

"You don't know me," I warn her. "My idea of fun could be scorpion breeding."

She searches my face for a long time and finally smiles. "I've seen you around. You don't do much, just sit in the shade and tap your fingers on the ground and listen to music. Sometimes you play air guitar," she adds. "You look pretty bored most of the time, like you're half asleep. But you seem harmless enough. And you're cute."

I stare back at her. So she *has* noticed me noticing her. And according to her I come off as boring and harmless. I wonder if that's how all women perceive me. Well, at least she threw *cute* in there.

"I can meet you here in an hour," I hear myself say. I wish I could catch the words and reel them back in my mouth to safely store away in my Shut the Hell Up, You Idiot file. What am I going to do with her? But before I can take the offer back, she nods.

"Perfect. I'll finish my courtyard collage." I look around at the dried grass, the cement benches, the scrawny trees and dusty ground. She's going to spend an hour photographing this eyesore? I sigh and head toward the English building, already contemplating an escape plan.

# Dylan

*I sit down on the dry, prickly grass* and watch him curiously as he dives inside the English building like he's running for cover.

My photography class has taught me two crucial lessons about life. First, become an avid people watcher. It's amazing the truth people expose when they think nobody's looking. Two, look for beauty where it isn't obvious. Try to see life through a creative lens. I love this challenge. Anyone can see what's right in front of them, but it's subtle beauty, the kind that takes time to discover, that you have to uncover and dust off, that catches my eye. I find things with cracks and flaws and textures so much more interesting than something polished and perfect and pristine. It's the same way with people.

I've taken my professor's advice and every day after class I people watch for one hour and collect observations. A camera's a lot like a journal: it can store feelings and emotions and stories if you take the time to record them. That's when I noticed this guy. It's easy to overlook him; his back is always molded to the side of the building like he's part statue. I almost doubted he was alive until one day when our eyes accidentally crossed paths. Even from across the courtyard, I could see they were a striking blue, the color of a late-afternoon sky (up close they're even more impressive—they can hold you hostage). But there's an edge to them that was more startling than the color. Instead of seeing, they were repelling. Deflecting. I tried smiling at him, but he didn't grin back at me. He didn't even nod—he just turned away like I had rudely stumbled into his line of vision.

He tries to blend in, which only makes him stand out to me. In the last two weeks, I've made a couple of observations:

1.  He never smiles. *Ever.* I've seen him nod to people who pass him on the sidewalk. He talks on his phone sometimes, and texts. He doesn't frown either. He's just emotionless. Numb. As if something's missing. Why doesn't this kid smile? Do his mouth muscles not work? Does he have braces? A gaping overbite? It's become my mission to make him smile—it's like trying to chip through a layer of ice to see if something's moving and flowing and alive underneath.

2.  He avoids people. This suggests a few theories—he's aloof, he's antisocial, or he has a contagious skin rash that he's afraid to spread. Or, the mostly likely scenario, he *chooses* to be alone. I think there's a reason

he prefers solitude over people, and I'm determined to figure out why. For me, life is one long expedition in search of the answers to *why*.

3.  He's cute, but not in a typical way. He's not one of the pretty boys that litter Phoenix like glittery ornaments. No tattoos, no spiky hair or muscle tank tops or shirts unbuttoned halfway down to expose bronzed skin and sun-streaked chest hair. This guy mostly wears gym shorts and baseball T-shirts and flip-flops. That's one thing we have in common. He's not trying to impress anyone. He may not be Mr. Approachable, but at least he's real.

4.  Music is his thing. It's always on. He zones out to it. And he always wears a hat. It's like he hides behind it, as if he's trying to escape or shut out the world.

I unzip my backpack and pull out my inspiration log (a hand-size journal I carry everywhere). I flip through the pages until I find my list of *oughtas* — weekly goals I assign to myself. In the year I've been making them, I've seen every single one through. This week's goal is Make a Friend. I squint out at the bright concrete and watch two girls walk through the courtyard, their high-heeled shoes clicking noisily on the sandy pavement. They glance in my direction and take in my jeans and my tennis shoes and I can almost hear the fashion police sirens wailing in the distance.

Make a Friend. This challenge is no easy feat, but I've been holding my own secret audition — listening to people's conversations and studying their mannerisms and waiting for someone intriguing to come along.

I look back at the English building and smile, because now I'm convinced.

This guy is perfect.

On the surface he might be callused, but looking through a creative lens, I see layers and textures. He reminds me of a folding chair, closed up and waiting to be shoved in a storage closet. I'm determined to see him unfold.

# ⅠⅠⅠ First Try ⅠⅠⅠ

## Gray

*Poetry is almost as bad as math*—a second language that only a select few can appreciate. I signed up for Creative Writing to get an English prerequisite out of the way. I also heard this professor was a stoned hippie and would pass a second-grader as long as he turned something in. I figured I'd just keep a journal and write a few autobiographical essays to coast through the elective. Now I'm forced to write poetry and think like a girl for four weeks, all poignant and deep and . . . pretty.

I sit down at the back of the room, fashionably four minutes late to class. Every class period we meet in small writing groups—groups of four and we're forced to awkwardly share our writing for measly participation points. We take turns reading our half-assed attempts out loud. I'm willing to bet most of us wrote in between classes or scribbled something lame over breakfast. One kid in my group actually wrote a love poem to sausage Mc-Muffins. Mrs. Stiller, our overly sensitive instructor, encourages us to be honest in our writing, to expose our inner secrets. Writing is a window into our souls, she preaches. I take the other route and keep it safe. I wrote about winning our state baseball game in high school. I wrote a poem about kayaking. It was crammed full of clichés and borrowed expressions. I tried to rhyme. It was humiliating.

After a half hour of brainstorming similes with a partner (mine texted her boyfriend the entire time, so I had to do all the work) and being assigned yet another poem (I'm beginning to think Creative Writing is a karmic punishment for something awful I did in a past life), class finally wraps up.

I shut my notebook with relief until I remember who's waiting for me outside. That annoying girl who up close, I have to admit, was cuter than I expected, but her weirdness overshadows her looks. I walk down the hall and consider taking the north exit doors, where coyote-girl can't see me and I can duck out to the parking lot and resume my safe afternoon plans of playing Madden Football. Then a thought eases my mind. Maybe she sat in the shade long enough for her brain to cool down so she can think rationally and realize it's rude—and probably dangerous—to bum rides off complete strangers.

She can't seriously think I want to be her friend. I give off all the warm welcomes of a Keep Out sign.

But when I walk outside, there she is, sitting in the grass and grinning up at me like I should be excited to see her. I acknowledge her with a single nod and head straight for the parking lot. She slings a red backpack over her shoulder and half skips, half springs across the courtyard to catch up to me.

She slows down and walks close to my side, too close, as if we're friends. I inch away onto the grass and tug the rim of my cap lower on my forehead.

"So, what's your story?" she asks as we walk to my car.

"I don't have a story," I grumble.

"Everyone has a story. At the end of the day, you do something," she says.

I open the passenger door of my hatchback to let the confined air escape. I walk to the other side and open the driver door, careful to avoid touching the metal handle since it would scorch my fingers. We stand there for a minute, facing each other across the car, waiting for the air inside to cool down to a degree below Hell. Being a slight coward, I turn the question back to her and ask what her story is.

"It always changes," she says. "These days, I'm a novice photographer." She catches a piece of loose hair and tucks it behind her ear.

I widen my eyes with mock surprise. "Oh, you're only a novice? You mean, you weren't professionally hired to capture the stunning cement courtyard?" I slump down in the car and she sits next to me. We're both quiet for a few seconds while we suffer in the heat.

"Sarcastic. Good to know," she says thoughtfully, as if she's tallying observations about me.

I grab my water bottle and take a swig from it. When I'm finished she reaches over, without asking, takes it out of my hand, and helps herself to a drink. So I'm your tour guide, chauffeur, and beverage provider? I shake my head and start the car, blasting the air conditioning. It feels like a furnace blowing heat in our faces, but at least it gets the air moving. She makes herself at home, stretching her skinny legs out and resting a dirty sneaker on top of my dashboard. I raise an eyebrow at her sneaker and ask her if she's comfortable or if she'd like a pillow or maybe a strawberry margarita.

She thanks me but tells me no, she's just fine, and I tighten my lips together to fight a smile because I won't give her the satisfaction of thinking she's amusing me. We pull out of the parking lot and I drive toward Tempe, a town close to Mesa and Scottsdale — suburbs that make up the sprawling metropolis of Phoenix.

She rambles on, telling me she doesn't have a story yet. That's why she drove out here for the summer, to find one. She tells me life is a story. We can make it a Harlequin romance, a mystery, a memoir. We can make it pamphlet-size or an ongoing series.

"I want mine to be exceptional," she says. I tell her good luck with that.

"How long have you been playing guitar?" she suddenly asks, and again I question this girl's sanity. Am I escorting my stalker on a tour of the city?

"How'd you know that?"

She shrugs at my inquiry, as if it's obvious. "Your hands," she says. "The fingertips on your left hand are callused."

I stare down at my hands, impressed with her observation. There are rough calluses on the tips of each finger from hours of practice—one of them is starting to peel away. If she weren't sitting next to me, I'd chew it off.

She studies my hands. "It looks like you've been playing a lot," she notes. I don't argue because she's right. I've been playing more than I care to admit—four to six hours a day. It's a little sad that my closest relationship in life is with a guitar. It's an escape, a way to avoid my parents.

I look back at her and imagine her analyzing thoughts (a superpower all women appear to be born with). *He has no ambition. Or maybe he has no friends.* Earlier today I'd thought her eyes were brown, but now I notice they're layered—dark brown on the outside, golden brown inside, and an unmistakable ring of bluish-green near the center. Her brown hair has tints of red in it, when the sun catches it right. She has dots of freckles on her nose and a dimple in her left cheek. Her front bottom teeth are a little crooked. She doesn't wear any makeup that I can see, except for Chap Stick that she's now applying over her dry pink lips. She always looked ordinary from a distance, even odd. But as I gaze at her now, there's something about her that's striking.

"What's your name?" I ask her, because for the first time I want to know. She grins at me and her one dimple stands out.

"Dylan," she says.

"Dylan," I test the word on my tongue. "I'm Gray."

I half expect her to already know this about me, but her eyebrows crease in puzzlement.

"What's your first name?"

I roll my eyes. "That is my first name. Who introduces themselves by their last name?"

She argues that plenty of people do, like James Bond, and doctors, and she's pretty sure in some remote villages in northern England they still do, places where they wear smoking jackets with elbow pads and wool bowler hats.

What the hell is she talking about? I just frown and point out that none of those examples relates to the current situation.

Dylan insists on knowing the history behind my name. I sigh and recount the story for the hundredth time. My mom named me Gray, I tell her, because she's from the northern coast of Oregon, where it rains every single day. The sky is a continual gray. The ocean, the ground—even the air is saturated in thick gray fog. She named me Gray because it reminds her of home. I thought I'd grow into the name, but I hate having to assure people that my mom made this decision in a marijuana-free state of mind. Dylan tells me she loves it. It's unique. Girls have always liked my name. I guess that's a bonus.

"Gray," she says. "Blue-eyed Gray."

"So, where do you want to go?" I ask to get the subject off me.

"Anywhere," she offers. "I want to see everything."

I thank her for narrowing down the options and decide to take her where every girl in the city flocks—Mill Avenue. I promise

Dylan its blocks provide endless boutiques stocked with jeans that cost more than some people's rent, restaurants with linen napkins and second-story verandas so people can look down on the world while they enjoy a thirty-dollar bowl of lettuce, and coffee shops that sell certified organic, free trade, gourmet, locally roasted, freshly brewed, gold-infused coffee (I'm not sure about the gold-infused part, but I wouldn't be surprised). One cup. Five bucks. Savor the taste of a liquid rip-off.

I pull up to the curb and park alongside a sushi restaurant with outdoor seating. We look out the window at groups of couples meeting for a late lunch, enjoying mists of water spraying continuously overhead to relieve the cooking stale air around them and to create a cooler Mediterranean climate for their dining experience. The women wear huge bug-eye sunglasses and the men fondle their BlackBerries.

Dylan turns to me and waits. I nod toward the street and tell her to have fun. "I'll meet you back here in an hour," I say. I figure she can blow money galore while I hide in the shade. Her face falls, and the disappointment in her eyes makes me give in and agree to walk a few blocks.

We head down the sidewalk and her camera bounces against her chest, hanging around her neck from a black cord. I want to point out she looks like a tourist, but from my brief observations of this girl one thing is evident: she couldn't care less what people think of her. Few people are born with a judgment-proof shield that repels critical looks. Dylan's shield is pretty thick.

We peruse store windows trying to lure us with sale signs and racks of clothes. I expect Dylan to dive inside, but she's more interested in people watching. Lines of grubby vagabonds and weary travelers line the street, begging for food and money. Some play beat-up instruments, some have skinny dogs lying around their feet. It always amazes me that homeless people have dogs. If they can barely feed themselves, what kind of scraps are their pets eating? On second thought, I don't want to know.

While we walk she asks me questions. Not your standard interview questions, like *What are you studying?* or *Where do you work?* or *Where did you grow up?* I don't know where she pulls these from. *Do you think the army should start training for intergalactic warfare? Who invented liquid butter and why? Does anyone actually find wool clothing comfortable?* We're arguing about the pros and cons of leaf blowers when I check my phone and realize we've been walking for almost an hour.

On the street, shiny convertibles parade by and determined shoppers weave around us, reeking of perfume and cologne, their hands pressed protectively around purses and bags.

We pass a homeless man holding up a sign that asks CAN I HAVE A JOINT? I lean toward Dylan and whisper, "At least he's honest."

Dylan stops and asks to take his picture. He nods and she takes a few shots while I watch from the side. She asks the man where he's from and, to my surprise, he sounds competent. His blue eyes are bright and his silver hair is tied back in a ponytail that runs halfway down his back. He tells us he hitchhiked from Colorado, where he was working on an organic farm. He tells us he has a college degree but he hates the Man, because the Man invented the System, which invented Capitalism, which invented Consumerism, which is destroying Mother Earth. He's never paid taxes but he's never stolen a thing in his life. He lives one day at a time, he says. He lives better than most people. He smiles a goofy grin at us, gaping with missing teeth.

Dylan hands me her camera and asks me to wait a minute while she sprints inside a swimsuit store. I stand outside next to the bum and stare at the ground. Now she gets the sudden impulse to shop? Two minutes later, Dylan runs back holding a pair of blue flip-flops. She hands them to the shoeless man and asks him what his name is. He looks surprised, and then he grins and tells her it's Sam.

"Here, Sam," she says. "I think these will fit." He grabs the sandals and sticks his brown toes between the thongs. He nods and thanks her. He calls her an angel. I raise an eyebrow at the compliment. I still vote for "crazy" as a fitting description.

We continue down the street and Dylan stops only to catch photographs of people when they're too distracted to notice. She snaps a picture of a mother and three daughters who are window shopping, all wearing matching pink capri pants with bright white tennis shoes. "Team Capri," she whispers to me.

I almost smile, and just when I discover I'm enjoying myself, I catch sight of someone down the block. Standing under the shade of an awning is my old high school best friend, Brandon Stack, with a tall blonde. He waves and my mouth tightens into a frown. I knew he still lives in Phoenix; he got a full ride to play baseball at Arizona State. I exhale sharply and walk toward him. Brandon extends his hand and thumps his fist against mine.

"Dude, it's great to see you," he says. I nod but I don't recip-rocate the feeling. The timing sucks. Brandon can't help who he is—a physical reminder of what my life is and more important what it *isn't*. I spent so much time carefully packing up my past. Sealing it shut. Storing it away. Seeing Brandon makes that box fall open and all the memories spill out at my feet.

Dylan leans against the building in the shade, next to the blond bombshell. She looks like a shabby street kid standing next to a sparkling celebrity.

"Oh," Brandon says. "This is my girlfriend, Kim." I reach out my hand to shake Kim's, and she looks up from her cell phone long enough to make eye contact. She offers me a limp handshake in return. Her bright white teeth greet me through pink shiny lips, and her blue eyes meet mine under a black coat of mascara. I gawk at her because I'm a guy and it's what we do when women dress like they're hoping to be discovered by Victoria's Secret. Kim is universally beautiful. Platinum blond. Breasts the size of dodge balls, spilling out of a bright blue tube top. A silver hoop is pierced through her tan belly button. She could be a *Playboy* centerfold, but she knows it, which makes her off-limits to the average guy. Brandon used to go for tomboys, or for the quirky, funny girls that made him laugh. He always claimed looks didn't matter. This girl is proof he sold out.

I look back at Brandon, and even though we haven't spoken in months, I know his life is the same (other than his new supermodel sidekick). When everything comes easily to you, it never challenges you to change. He was our high school homecoming king, starting shortstop of our state-winning baseball team. Good grades. Charismatic. Worshiped. He even has looks on his side. Rumor has it he'll be the starting shortstop at ASU as a freshman.

I introduce him to Dylan, and she nods and offers a half-grin but doesn't extend her hand. She keeps her fingers tucked inside her pockets, and I notice her eyes narrow as they pass between Brandon and me.

Brandon quickly looks her up and down. He glances back at me, skeptically. I don't blame him. She's dressed for yard work, and in Phoenix, looks define you. His face turns serious and my stomach buckles. *Oh, no. Please don't go there. Not right now.*

## Dylan

*I lean against the brick building* and watch the tension rise between Brandon and Gray. It's so thick, I could wrap my fingers around the air and wring it out. I'm tempted to try.

The Brooklyn Decker clone next to me adjusts her tube top and sighs. I noticed Gray drooling over Kim when he shook her hand. I can't really blame him. Kim has the face for a billboard and her body curves like a human hourglass, but I'm not intimidated and here's why: The first thing I notice about people are their eyes. It gives them away. You can tell how alive they are. How genuine. How deep they feel and how much they wonder. Kim's eyes are dull and glazed over like they're empty, like she doesn't really see people. She just sees herself.

"How's your family handling things?" Brandon asks, and his question snaps my attention back. I notice Gray's face instantly harden.

"Fine," he says, but his throat sounds constricted as if he has to force out the words. "We're doing fine."

"Is your mom okay?" Brandon asks.

He nods quickly. "Yeah. I mean, it's been hard, but she's dealing."

"You thinking about playing baseball again?" he asks.

Gray concentrates on the ground and kicks at an imaginary rock.

"Oh, I don't know," he says.

"I'm playing in town this summer. If you ever want to practice, you should give me a call. We could hang out."

"That sounds good," he mumbles. He's a terrible liar.

"You doing okay?" Brandon asks. I see Gray's hands clench into fists, and it makes my back straighten up.

"Yeah, considering. Who knows, maybe I'll be at ASU this year. I can check out a game."

There's jealousy on his face, as if Brandon stole a dream he feels entitled to. Or, maybe it's Brandon's life in general: college, baseball, aspiring porn star girlfriend.

"Great," Brandon says. "I can get you front-row seats."

Gray grinds his teeth together and nods. "Sounds great," he mumbles.

*Right,* I think as I watch his bitter expression. *That sounds super.*

We all stand there silently for a few seconds. Kim blows a bubble with her gum and pops it between her teeth—her one contribution to the conversation. Gray shifts his weight back and forth on his feet as if he wants to run, and without thinking, I step forward and tug on his hand. He turns to me and looks down at our hands with surprise, and I say the first thing that pops into my head.

"Aren't you going to tell him the news?" I ask.

"What news?" he asks, wide-eyed, like he fears the response.

I offer Brandon an apologetic smile. "I doubt Gray's going to be at ASU this fall," I tell him, and glance over at Gray. "I mean, Duke just accepted you."

Brandon's eyebrows fly up. "Really? Out east? That's awesome."

Gray blinks back at him.

"And what about Stanford?" I add. "You can't turn down a full-ride academic scholarship. Besides, there's a lot more to life than baseball." I smile victoriously back at Brandon.

"Yeah," Gray says. "We'll see."

"It was great to meet you," I say, and pull Gray down the street. Brandon waves goodbye to us, his face frozen with surprise. Kim doesn't look up; she's busy inspecting her manicure for signs of distress. We're a block away before I let go of his hand, hot inside mine. He still looks angry, but there's a hint of relief in his eyes, even a little amusement.

"You know," he says, "you should come equipped with a warning button that lights up when you're about to say something ridiculous. That way people can run before absurdity strikes."

"Thanks," I say with a smile. It's the first compliment he's given me, and it's a good one.

He frowns at my beaming face and informs me that it wasn't a compliment. "Why did you say that?"

I look away while I decide how to answer this. Saying I was helping him out would only annoy him. Gray doesn't seem like the type who appreciates emotional charity.

"I think you should know right away that I have a rare medical condition," I confess.

He doesn't look at all surprised to hear this. He watches me closely and waits.

"I suffer from freak creative outbursts," I say, which is true, and his mouth starts to twitch.

"That's what you call *lying?*"

"No," I refute. "*Lying* is manipulation. I prefer to call what I did 'improvisation in times of desperation.'"

"Excuse me?"

I throw my hands up in the air. So much for my rare medical condition. "I was trying to help you out. You were getting ready to punch him," I say.

He glares at me for making an accurate observation. "No, I wasn't."

"Your hands were balled up in fists," I remind him. "And you were grinding your teeth together. I wouldn't call that friendly body language."

"You don't miss much, do you?"

I shake my head. "Look, I'm sorry I lied. I was trying to save your knuckles."

And just like that, Gray smiles. It makes his eyes light up. It changes his entire face. I can see the layers of ice beginning to melt away. Wow, I think. This guy needs to smile more often.

"Duke and Stanford?" he asks, still smiling. "Why not Harvard? Are you trying to lowball my intelligence?"

We start walking and I ask if he's mad and he shakes his head. He tells me he's just annoyed that his past caught up with him on Mill Avenue of all places. I nod, but I know what's really bothering him—that an overly perceptive girl he barely knows was there to witness it.

He looks at me and grins again, and I know it's his way of saying thanks. We're both silent as we reach the end of the street, where it dissolves into a city park along the edge of Tempe Town Lake, a shiny jewel of water with a tall bridge built on top of it like a crown. Geckos run around our feet and I walk down the grassy hill to the lake. Gray follows behind me and I turn to see him watching me like he's waiting for something.

"What?" I ask.

"Aren't you going to ask me what that was all about?" he asks.

I study him. His mouth looks bolted shut with a dozen locks. "No," I say simply. "You don't look like you're aching to talk about it." Gray exhales a long breath of relief and shakes his head. I don't pry any further. I lift my camera and aim it at the calm water, mirroring the sky. The shutter clicks when I take the picture.

"I should take you home," he says.

I nod, but first, I need to capture a memory. I want to freeze my favorite part of this day. I turn and focus the lens on Gray and take a shot of his profile before he can turn away.

"Hey," he says, and tries to block the camera with his hand. He tells me he never agreed to a photo shoot, but he's grinning again and his eyes are lighter. That's three smiles in five minutes.

I feel like I deserve a medal. Sometimes the smallest victories in life are more rewarding than the greatest milestones.

\* \* \* \* \*

*Gray drives me home and I point out directions* to a sprawling estate in a gated community in Scottsdale.

"Are you kidding me?" he asks as we drive by homes that look large enough to be hotels. I tell him to turn into a driveway leading to a three-car garage, and he asks me what kind of trust fund I recently inherited.

"Not what you expected?"

He stares down at my baggy, faded jeans. "You dress like you should be pitching a tent in a state park." He cuts himself off as if worried he's offended me. "You just don't seem . . . I don't know. Materialistic."

"I'm not, but my aunt got a nice divorce settlement. Plastic surgeons must do pretty well in Phoenix." Gray smirks and we look at the house, which appears to be three homes glued together, perfect for a family of twenty. He notices the beat-up orange Volvo station wagon parked next to us. The bumpers are covered with rust and the paint is warped and peeling.

"Looks like her car could use a face-lift," he says.

"That's my beast. His name's Pickle."

He wrinkles his eyebrows at the orange car.

"I see the resemblance," he says, and points to my Wisconsin license plate. "You're a long way from home."

I nod. "That's the idea." I open the door but I stall before getting out—one foot's on the driveway and the other's still lingering in his car like it doesn't want to move. "Can we do this again tomorrow?" I ask easily, as if we're already friends. Because

I feel like we are. From Gray's stunned expression, he doesn't agree.

"Do what?"

"Explore the city." I tell him maybe we can avoid Mill Avenue. "I'm glad I got to see it, but those people take themselves way too seriously. I feel like you need to be on a guest list just to walk into some of those stores."

"Welcome to Phoenix," he says. He stares back at me with stubborn eyes, like I picked the wrong local if I'm looking for excitement, but I return the look because I think he's wrong. He has a venturous side, I can sense it, but for some reason it's buried.

"Listen, Dylan, I don't do a whole lot. I don't think I'm the guy for you."

I smile at him. "Of course you are," I say, and hop out before he can argue. "See you tomorrow."

I take long, confident strides toward the giant, shiny oak door, past manicured trees and shrubs and a lawn that manages to be lush with thick green grass in the dry desert heat. In my baggy jeans and messy hair, I know I don't fit into this plastic palace. But I don't want to fit in. That's when no one notices you. You leave a longer impression when you're brave enough to stand out.

# ⅠⅠⅠ First Challenge ⅠⅠⅠ

## Gray

*I walk out the front doors* of the English building the next afternoon and there she is, sitting on a bench in the courtyard, her camera adorning her neck, quick to access, like she's a paparazzo waiting to snag a photo of a celebrity student. She's wearing her usual black tennis shoes, but today she has on green hiking shorts with gray socks pulled up to her knees. When she sees me, she jumps up and sprints to my side before I even reach the sidewalk. I blink at her, still half asleep from class. Her presence jolts me awake like an alarm clock, and I'm not exactly happy about it.

"Normal people slow down when it's this hot," I inform her.

"Do you have plans today?" she asks, her eyes wild. Before I can formulate an excuse, she nods. "That's what I thought."

She grabs my hand in hers and swings them back and forth as if we're childhood best friends. She pulls me toward her car and informs me that she took over the job of itinerary coordinator because I lack the necessary enthusiasm. Then she announces we're going on a hike. I yank my hand out of hers and tell her she's nuts.

"It's eight hundred degrees out," I say. "Have you ever heard of heat stroke?" She smiles and informs me that we'll be fine, that she brought sunscreen. I decide there's no point in talking common sense to this girl. She doesn't speak the language.

She unlocks the door of her rusted jalopy wagon.

"Live a little," she tells me. "You're never going to experience anything if you wait around for perfect conditions. Look at the sky, Gray. It's gorgeous. It's perfect right now, and you're missing it."

I squint up at the stark blue sky. There isn't a trace of a cloud, just a deep blue abyss spread above us.

"And it's only a hundred and five degrees," she adds. I reluctantly sit down in the trapped heat of her car. We pull out of the parking lot and the pedals squeak when Dylan presses down on the clutch. The black leather gearshift is worn smooth, and the car rattles defiantly as if the engine is going to explode when we accelerate onto the highway.

"Pickle doesn't like going over fifty-five," Dylan explains. I stare at her and raise my eyebrows. She informs me Pickle's favorite music is oldies, he gets along best with Ford makes and models and he prefers to brake rather than accelerate. She lightly presses her foot on the brake and Pickle immediately hums in response. "See?" she says with a knowing smile.

I let out a long sigh. I can't believe we're having a conversation about her car's preferred music taste and driving style. I can't believe she tricked me into spending another day with her. I have a life, I want to tell her. I have four episodes of *Myth Busters* to catch up on. Okay, I don't have a life.

I look out the window at a range of rolling brown hills in the distance. The word *Arizona* is written on one of the peaks in white capital letters.

"Why do people write on the mountains out here?" Dylan asks me over Pickle's loud rattling.

"Because they can," I say.

Her eyes narrow. "It doesn't mean they should. It looks like giant piles of bird poop smeared into letters."

"I guess you could look at it that way. I see it as white paint."

"If you could write one word on a mountain for everybody to see, what would you write?" Is she capable of a serious conversation?

"Are you capable of a serious conversation?"

She looks me straight in the eye and insists that this is *very* serious.

"That's a tough one," I finally say.

Her eyes perk up to discover we agree on something. "I know! There are so many great words, like *intrigue* and *scintillating* and *serendipity* and *indecorous* and *cataclysmically*."

"*Cata*-what?"

"But there are also some terrible words," she continues. "Like *membrane*. And *moist*. And *protoplasm*." She emphasizes this point by pretending to vomit next to me. I look over and pretend to be grossed out by the imaginary vomit.

Dylan continues to banter as we head south, and her voice starts to relax me because it's a distraction. I stretch my legs out and lift my face to the window to catch the hot desert breeze. I rest my dirty tennis shoes on Pickle's dashboard, and I'm comfortable. I can't help but grin to myself, because I realize Dylan wasn't being rude yesterday. She was just being herself. Why bother asking somebody permission to be yourself?

She talks about the photography class she's taking at Mesa. It's her Aunt Diane's idea, she says, to give her something to do for the summer. She's housesitting while her aunt's traveling to art shows around the country, and she's helping out with house projects to make money, mostly painting jobs. She tells me her aunt's recently divorced and recently out of the closet. Dylan claims she knew all along, ever since a family reunion when Dylan was in middle school. Aunt Diane (Aunt Dan, as she's now referred to lovingly by her family) spent the entire reunion trying to coordinate a women-only rugby match. A dead giveaway, Dylan claims. She also owns one too many pairs of those khaki hiking pants that can zip off at the knee and become shorts. To my surprise, I'm laughing.

We exit the highway for Picacho Peak State Park, and desolate dry hills surround us. It isn't much of a park. It looks like a barren, dusty terrain full of tumbleweeds. We curve along a winding blacktop road until we come to a deserted parking lot. A small state park sign welcomes us, faded in the baking sunlight.

Her car door squeaks open as if it's screaming in pain (Pickle has arthritic joints, Dylan claims). She tosses some water bottles in her backpack and checks her film supply, and we head up a rocky trail. The highway is still visible from the park—the scrubby desert bushes and cactus leave miles of visibility in every direction, and the roar of semi engines in the distance compete with the noisy humming of cicadas.

Dylan talks about her assignment as we head up a winding trail. She has to pick one stationary object and capture it from four different angles. In class, they'll dye these four images different colors. The point is to show how stepping around things and taking the time to see them from different perspectives changes their entire image. Her dad gave her his old manual camera for the summer. She tells me about shutter speed and backlighting, framing and focusing.

While we hike, we discover the unique beauty of this state park—it's home to a sprawling community of saguaros. These cactuses are Arizona's mascot; they grow to be hundreds of years old and their green, prickly stems look like arms reaching out to the sun. We walk up to a saguaro with a gaping wound in its side, as if a giant bent down and took a huge bite out of its green flesh. Its skeleton is exposed—a core of long, vertical beams of tan wood. Dylan stops to examine it and I stand next to her.

"It's dying," I say. "When the center is exposed like that, it doesn't have a chance."

"But it's beautiful," she points out. I stare at the shriveling cactus and try to see the beauty in it. "That's the way I want to go out," she decides.

"What?" I ask. "Torn up and ripped open?"

She shakes her head. "Totally exposed, with no regrets. You can tell this cactus lived; it has the battle scars to prove it. Why go out looking perfect and put together? It means you didn't experience anything. You didn't take any risks."

I walk around it and Dylan follows me, snapping pictures. When she isn't looking, while her focus is concentrated on finding the perfect frame, I steal glances at her. She seems different today. Almost graceful. Her tall, gangly body ducks and crouches, and my eyes are drawn to her movements. I watch her back and neck curl into a squat. I notice her long fingers, with silver rings twinkling in the sun. I watch the muscles tighten on her slender arms, where thin bracelets clang from her movements.

We analyze what the cactuses are doing. She points out a cactus that's dancing and one that's praying. I point out a cactus with all of its fingerly stems curled over, except for the middle one, which is sticking straight up in the air.

"It's flipping us off," I say. She stands next to me and studies the middle finger, stretched out proud and defiant toward the freeway in the distance.

"You must feel a special connection with this one," she says.

She snaps a picture and looks over at me with a smile. She's smiled a hundred times today, but this one is different. It fills her eyes. It makes my breath catch. I look away and drain the bottle of water. The heat must be messing with my head.

She turns and steps back on the path, but I stand with my feet planted, mentally trying to coach my feelings into being reasonable. I can't actually like this girl. She's too random. She sprawls out on public sidewalks and makes friends with homeless people. She insists her car has a personality. She thinks cactuses move like people. But few people surprise me. And my eyes linger on her body and my mind lingers on her words. I can't deny that. I internally store this realization in my Oh, Shit file.

I don't want to feel anything toward Dylan. It's safer to stay numb.

# Dylan

*We loop around the trail and head back* to the parking lot, where Pickle is waiting for us in the gravel yard. I open up a cooler and two floating sandwiches slosh back and forth in the melted ice water. I inspect the baggies and they're still sealed, so I hand Gray a sandwich and a soda. I grab a bag of chips and a pack of licorice, and we sit on top of a picnic table with our legs crossed and look out at the desert plain.

Gray takes off his hat and runs his fingers through damp, curly hair that's so dark, it's almost black. It's thick and jumps out in all directions, as if to celebrate a rare moment of freedom. It makes his eyes stand out.

"So," I say. "You helped me with my assignment. Now let me help you with one of yours."

He wipes his mouth with the back of his hand and chews on his sandwich. He takes a long drink before he answers me as if he's contemplating whether or not to open up, no matter how casual the topic. Finally he says he's stuck in a poetry unit and it isn't exactly his strength.

"How can you say it isn't your strength?"

"Because it's poetry," he says, like it's some kind of stomach flu.

"It's the only style of writing where you can break all the rules," I say. "It's so liberating."

He chews on his sandwich and considers this. A gust of wind blows his hair over his forehead. "Yeah, but you have to use metaphors and personification and all that crap."

"Crap?" I argue. "It's just sewing words together. Random words in any order. It doesn't even have to mean anything. It just has to mean something to you."

He smirks and explains this one has to mean something. He tells me he has to write a descriptive poem. I take a bite of licorice and tell him it sounds like my photography assignment but with words. I point out the hills around us.

"You could describe a saguaro," I offer.

He finishes his sandwich and grins. "Yeah, a poem about a cactus. How original. Maybe my mom will tape it to the fridge next to the one I wrote in preschool."

I unzip my bag and pull out my inspiration log. Gray notices some words scribbled on the front cover. He scoots closer so he can see, and reads out loud:

"Normal: Conforming to the average or standard type. Weird: Odd, eccentric, suggesting the supernatural."

He meets my eyes and I smile. He leans away and studies me for a few seconds, as if he still doubts my planet of origin. It's a common reaction from people, since most of my functioning brain cells are programmed for random thoughts.

"Did you make up those definitions?" he asks. I shake my head and tell him I looked them up. He doesn't have to ask which definition characterizes me. It's also easy to see which category he currently fits into, and he looks insulted.

"You know, being normal isn't a terrible thing," he says.

"It isn't *terrible*," I agree. "It's just a lack of courage." He narrows his eyes and I point down at the cover. "You have to admit, one of those words sounds a little bit more exciting. Which way do you want to live your life?"

He glances back at the definitions. "It's something to think about," he says. Then his eyes move up, but slowly this time. I noticed Gray's starting to look at me today. Really look at me. Sometimes his eyes linger.

I uncap a pen and open up to a blank page and start to write. Strands of hair blow into my eyes and I brush them away. I hand the journal to Gray, and he tries to decipher my small, messy penmanship.

"I think too fast for my hand to keep up," I inform him. He reads the line out loud.

"'Ode to the Mighty Green Ones.'" He sets the journal down and I nod for him to continue.

"Am I supposed to do something?" he asks.

"It's the title of your poem. We'll take turns writing it, line by line."

I wait for him to say forget it, but he picks up the pen. He throws a few chips in his mouth and starts writing. He tosses the journal back at me, and his writing is clear and neat and legible — the opposite of mine. I shout his words into the wind, and it makes him jump with surprise.

"My Phoenix cactus," I yell, and clench my fist in the air for dramatic emphasis. I look over at Gray and nod. "That's a solid start."

This goes on for an hour. We scratch out lines; we take turns standing on the picnic table and reciting our poem to the family of cactuses around us for approval. I try sneaking the words *phallic* and *erect* into his poem, since saguaros are the most phallic plants I've ever seen, but he points out his classmates will read this and he doesn't want to sound like he has an obsession with the male anatomy.

"Oh, fine," I say.

# Gray

*I ask Dylan to stop by my house* on the way into town so I can grab my work shirt. The hours flew by and I'm going to be late for my evening shift. We pull into my driveway just as my mom's getting the mail. She stares with disbelief as Dylan's car sputters and wheezes to a stop.

"Does Pickle have emphysema?" I ask, and Dylan looks horrified I can suggest such a thing.

When my mom notices me in the passenger seat, her tired face softens.

"She's pretty," Dylan whispers. "She has your blue eyes."

I tighten my lips and open the car door. I hadn't planned on making introductions, but Dylan takes care of it for me. She kills the engine, to Pickle's relief, and jumps up to grab my mom's hand and give her arm a solid pump. My mom looks startled, and she offers a confused grin.

"Nice to meet you, Dylan," she says, and then turns to face me. Her eyes are glassy, as if she's recently been crying, but this is such a normal look for her that I've stopped wondering what's wrong.

"I have conferences so I'm leaving in a few minutes," she tells me. "Dad's flight is getting in late, so you're on your own tonight."

She meets Dylan's eyes and Dylan sees this as an invitation to share her life story. She explains she's in town for the summer and she met me at school. She tells my mom I'm a talented poet with a lot of potential. I'm amazed because Dylan's spoken more words to my mom in five minutes than I've spoken to her in a week. My mom looks equally surprised. She turns to me and asks me what my plans are for dinner, and I tell her I'm running late for work so I'll grab something out. Her eyes stare through me while I speak.

"Great. You can warm up leftovers for dinner," she says. I glance at Dylan to see if she caught this and her eyes meet mine for a split second to confirm that yes, she did. Of course she did. My mom says goodbye and we watch her disappear into the garage.

"She seems sad," Dylan says quietly.

"She has a lot on her mind," I say and she faces me.

"Do you have any brothers or sisters?"

"No," I say quickly, and shove my water bottle in my bag. I can feel her watching me, and I want to tell her that unending curiosity can be extremely annoying.

"You're mysterious, Gray," she tells me. I shrug and take my iPod out of my pocket.

"I think that's why I like you," she grins, reaching out and squeezing my arm. I feel my face redden and instinctively back up out of her reach.

I turn to glance at her once more before I head inside. She's leaning against her car, her ankles crossed, a thoughtful look on her face. Both her hands are tucked into the front pockets of her shorts. She looks at me and grins again, and I feel something twitch inside my stomach. It has to be hunger pains.

\* \* \* \* \*

*I can't sleep tonight.* The moon is full and it makes my feet shift and shuffle restlessly under the sheets. My thoughts are chasing me.

She's not my type. She's bizarre and awkward and she dresses like one of the bums on Mill Ave. But, that's the problem. She isn't awkward at all. She's a tomboy. And she dresses normal. She doesn't expose every piece of flesh to the world. And she isn't weird. She just doesn't go out of her way to impress people, which is impressive. And admit it: she's sexy.

I roll over onto my back and stare at the ceiling. I replay the faces of other girls in my memory. Girls I used to think were gorgeous. What did I find attractive about them? I can't remember. They're all artificial, too perfect, too similar, like cardboard cutouts molded into plastic shapes and sizes. They don't have the crease between their eyes when their imaginations are hard at work the way Dylan does. They all have blue or brown eyes, not Dylan's, with colors pooling together like swirls of paint blending in a drip of water. They don't have her busy hands and bouncy walk.

Most of all, they don't have Dylan's mind. They don't ask questions, don't explore the beauty hiding in sidewalk cracks or in lonely desert hills. They're too busy obsessing over themselves. They take themselves so seriously, and it contaminates the energy around them, because in their presence, I'm more self-conscious. I become sterile as I try to hide all my imperfections along with them. And that's a waste of time.

* * * * *

*I look for Dylan after class* the next day and find her spread out on the dry grass under the sparse shade of a tree. She has baggy jeans on again, and an army camouflage T-shirt with a white peace sign stenciled on the front. Her hair is tied back in a blue bandanna. I approach her because it feels natural.

"Want to grab lunch?" I ask quickly. It's not a date, I want to add. "Unless you have some peace rally to go to," I say, nodding to her shirt.

She smirks and hands me a folded piece of paper. I stare at her curiously and open it. The message is scribbled in her unique writing style — half her letters written in cursive, half of them printed, and all of them messy.

*Hi, Gray. I thought I'd run into you. You look great today. Especially your hair. Oh, wait you're wearing a baseball cap.*

I look away from the letter long enough to glare at Dylan.

"Funny," I say. She nods with a knowing smile. I focus back on the note.

*So, during my photography class my teacher dared me to go a day without talking. Apparently, I'm too vocal. I accepted the challenge. I can't say a word all day. Want to grab lunch?*

I fold the paper and hand it back to her. She can't be serious.

"Are you serious?"

She doesn't look up. She focuses on drawing a picture of a Kokopelli on her sketchpad.

"Can't you go a day without doing something insane?"

Dylan opens a notebook lying next to her on the grass and flips to a blank page. She writes for a few seconds and hands it over to me, meeting my eyes for the first time. Her fingers brush mine as I take it, and the touch makes my stomach clench. I yank my arm away because the reaction caught me by surprise. I look down at the notebook.

*I try to do one random thing every day.*

I read her comment with a frown.

"Just one random thing?" I ask. I sit down next to her in the grass because I have to admit, I'm intrigued. "What did you do yesterday?"

While she writes, I think back to our hiking trip. Every second of it was random. How can she narrow it down to one thing? She hands the notebook back to me.

*I bought two magazines I've never read before.* Wrestle World *and* Good Housekeeping.

I don't have to ask why. I watch her write a single word.

*Perspective.*

I stare at Dylan and feel a tug on my heart, like she's holding a string attached to it and is giving it a yank. She reminds me of someone I used to love. Someone so incredibly original, I was positive no one else like her existed in the world.

# ||| FIRST LISTEN |||

## Dylan

*Gray takes me to his favorite place for Mexican food,* Taco Boys. He says he wants to introduce me to the local ethnic cuisine in Phoenix; he just hadn't anticipated my being mute as part of the experience.

When we get inside, I write down my order for a middle-aged woman standing behind the register. She studies me with a patient smile and assumes I'm deaf. She reads my order and gives me a sympathetic nod. And a free soda.

We sit in a booth, and while we wait for our food, Gray finds it only appropriate to teach me all the swear words he knows in sign language (which sums up ninety percent of his understanding of the language, he claims). He also knows the signs for *fart* and *baby Jesus*, both of which he learned in Sunday school (one from his teacher and one from his classmate), and he demonstrates each to me. By the time the food comes, between our collective knowledge we're able to sign the expressions, "I call bullshit on that one," "Pay up, bitch," and "Jesus loves you." I can only hope we'll have plenty of opportunities to use them.

When Gray starts to eat, I grab a spiral notebook out of my backpack and write for a minute before I hand it to him.

*I've been craving advice lately, a piece of wisdom to follow. I went to a book signing the other day for this travel writer. He's been around the world and met thousands of people. I asked him to give me advice on the meaning of life, and all he did was laugh and say, "You've got me!"*

Gray reads my comment and raises a single eyebrow. "Leave it to you to start a deep conversation right now," he says. "Your problem is you think too highly of people. I just want to be left alone."

I write down a single word and flip the notebook over so he can see.

*Why?*

He stares straight into my eyes—a level stare, as if I've just opened up a topic he'd rather avoid.

"You really want to know?" I nod slowly and he pauses to give me time to reconsider. Then he sucks in a deep breath. "People annoy the crap out of me," he says. "I think people are nervous and loud and rude and selfish and stupid pretty much all the time."

He watches me closely to gauge my reaction as if he's afraid I'll whack him with my notebook. But I feel myself grinning. I take a bite of my quesadilla and roll my hand to motion for him to continue. He doesn't hesitate this time.

"If they're beautiful they know it, so they don't bother having a personality or associating with people that don't fit into their league or can't afford their company. And, somehow these people are the most popular, which makes absolutely no sense. People try so hard to be accepted, they turn into a walking stereotype. They're pathetically easy to predict. They're insecure and try to mask it with whatever product corporate America is currently marketing. And they *always* let you down. Just give them enough time, and they will."

He meets my eyes again as if to warn me the flood gates are

open and now's my chance to run. Somehow I have the power to make him spill his mind.

"Want to know what else I think?"

I nod.

"I think everyone's caught up in these narrow-minded worlds and they think their world exists in the center of the universe. Relationships only happen when it's convenient. You have to walk on eggshells for people because that's about how strong they are these days. And you can't confront people, because if you do, that brittle shell of confidence will crack. So we all become passive cowards that carry a fake smile wherever we go because God forbid you let your guard down long enough for people to see your life isn't perfect. That you have a few flaws. Because who wants to see *that?*"

He takes a huge bite of his burrito to mark the end of this cheerful speech.

I write down a few words and slide the notebook across the table.

*Interesting theory. What's your conclusion?*

He meets my eyes. "My theory is everybody sucks. So, my conclusion is I don't need anybody."

I roll my eyes, which only encourages him.

"It's true," he says. "I have music. I have books. I have cable."

I say *bullshit* in sign language and he laughs.

"I'm fine with being alone," he insists. "I like the company I keep. Most people need constant distractions, because if they slow down long enough to evaluate their lives, it makes them internally combust. Like if you folded them inside out, you'd find a huge monster inside. A train wreck."

*Too much independence isn't a good thing,* I write.

I lean toward him over the table as he reads. He leans away.

"People will drive you crazy," he says, accentuating each word.

*Not having people in your life will drive you crazy, too.*

"I disagree," he says, and I start writing again. He smiles at my tenacity. I'm determined to change his mind and he's equally determined to fight me. I slide the journal across the table.

*Look around you. The earth wouldn't exist without the sun. Plants would die without rain. We're all meant to lean on something. Or someone.*

I smile. He frowns. He glances around the restaurant and eyes a table of girls watching us, probably listening to his slightly cynical rant. He surprises me and grabs the pen out of my hand. He starts writing something down in his neat block letters.

He slides the journal back to me.

*I build walls around myself. I lean on those.*

I don't need to ask him why. Everybody builds walls—it's for protection. Gray's are just higher and more reinforced than the average person's.

I scribble quickly. *Maybe you should break the walls down once in a while.* I look back to see the table of girls still watching us while he responds.

*I'll just build them up again,* he writes.

*But maybe you'll add a few windows the next time around. Or a door?*

He slides the journal back to me and speaks out loud. "You're strange. Has anyone ever told you that?"

*That's a compliment. I'd rather be noticed than blend in.*

"It's getting hard not to notice you," he says, and our eyes latch for a couple seconds until he looks away. I tap my pen on the table and write a single sentence. I push it over and watch him carefully. He looks down at my question.

*If someone gave you a magical eraser that could wipe out one thing in your past, what would it be?*

From his hard expression, I see I hit too close to a nerve. He pulls his baseball cap low over his eyes. It's his way of shutting me out. The topic's officially closed. He pushes the paper back and shakes his head.

"I don't want to go there," he says.

He finishes his burrito and nachos while I compose a letter to the manager of Taco Boys, expressing how much I loved my chicken quesadilla. It ends up being three pages long. I draw hearts and rainbows at the end, around one distinct signature, Gray Thomas. I show it to him with a proud smile and he just shakes his head. I hand the letter to the cashier before we leave.

Gray frowns at the clock on his dashboard when we get in the car—we spent more than two hours in Taco Boys. He tells me I have the power of making time disappear and it's going to make him late for work, again. He turns up the stereo and I lean my head back and look out the window at the dusty landscape and endless strip malls and it suddenly makes me crave water and trees and clouds and all the things this desert city lacks.

While we drive back to the Mesa CC parking lot, I write down another question.

*Tell me what I should know about Phoenix.*

He rattles off ideas that come to mind. He tells me the trick to surviving a summer in the desert is to dodge the sunshine. And avoid blacktop.

"Don't touch the metal clasp of your seat belt when you get in the car," he says. "You'll get third-degree burns. And don't bother looking for parking with shade. There isn't any."

He warns me not to run outside during the day. The air baking on the streets gets so hot, it can literally burn the inside of your throat and make it blister. Try not to walk farther than a block if you have to. Drive everywhere. Carry water. He recommends a gallon jug. It's a dry heat, so your sweat evaporates. You don't realize how much water you lose. You're always dehydrated.

He tells me to keep an eye on my car tires. The heat makes the rubber expand and tires can blow pretty easily. Keep the pressure low. Remember, rattlesnakes can't hear—that's why it's easy to sneak up on them. They sense by feeling vibrations. If you're on a sandy trail, throw a handful of rocks on the path to warn them you're coming. They'll slither away. The fear is mutual.

I start to write while he talks.

Don't worry about scorpions, he continues. They're around, but unless you're flipping over rocks on a hiking trail, you should be able to avoid them. Carry sunscreen wherever you go. And Chap Stick. Get a tattoo. Since I'm a girl, he suggests my lower back. For guys, he recommends the bicep, some kind of a tribal pattern. Dye your hair blond with even blonder highlights. Get a deep tan or spray your skin until it turns orange, because that looks *really* natural. Drive a convertible. Mustangs will make you instant friends. If you're the rugged type, buy a Jeep Wrangler. It's a lust magnet for any gender. Own sunglasses. Flashy ones, with the brand prominently displayed. If you don't have an outdoor pool where you live, know someone who does. Eat lots of sushi. It's satisfying without all the loaded calories. And reduce, reuse, recycle.

He pulls up next to Pickle in the parking lot.

"You're a really good listener," he points out.

I hand him my journal.

*Just one more question. Is there anything you like about living here?*

He studies my eyes and I get the impression there is something he likes. Or someone. His face breaks into a smile.

"Enough questions for one day," he says.

# ||| First Realize |||

## Gray

*I don't see her on campus the next day,* and I try to convince myself that I'm relieved to be spared a day from witnessing her "do one random thing." She still annoys me. A little.

But when I drive home, the luster of my life of cable, my life of walls, of solitude, has lost its appeal. It's hard to suddenly downshift your life once you realize you've acclimated to moving at a faster speed.

When she isn't there the following day, I start to wonder. And when she dares to disappear the third day, my spirit sinks all the way into my shoes. I drag them around campus.

I barely know this girl. But in our short time together, something inside of me has broken open. I stumbled on a treasure in the sandy courtyard of a community college. My eyes are starting to absorb the world around me instead of deflecting everyone and everything. Or maybe they're just on the lookout for one person. My body's beginning to creep out of its shell, and life, like a distant friend that's terrible at keeping in touch, has stumbled back onto my path and we're shaking hands, slowly attempting to catch up.

I sulk between classes, looking around campus for her, wondering when I'll see her again. What if her photography class is finished? The sessions are short in the summer—some are only one or two weeks. I slump down against the science building and panic. I don't have her number. I don't even know her last name.

I'm such an idiot. Why didn't I ask for her phone number?

* * * * *

*She isn't in the courtyard the next day either.* I bought her a pack of black-and-white film to surprise her in case she showed up. I scour the campus for the one girl wearing baggy jeans. I listen for her heavy tennis shoes brushing against the dry cement. I walk around the asphalt parking lot and scan the cars for Pickle, but all I discover is the ground is so hot I can feel the heat penetrate through my shoes until my feet burn. I could try to retrace my drive to her aunt's house, but I wasn't paying attention when I dropped her off. I even consider finding the photography professor and begging him to give me her last name.

I spend Creative Writing mentally kicking my own ass. Mrs. Stiller assigns an essay to write about a person who's recently made an impact on our lives. Seriously, this woman is my nemesis. I want to slide-tackle her for magnifying my mistake. While having to list characteristics of this heroic person, I realize with disgust that I wasn't even nice to Dylan. I spent half of the time avoiding her. I treated her like a scab I wanted to pick and flick off because lately I've grown so used to bleeding. And when I did open up to her, all I did was crap all over the world. What a fun guy. No wonder she stopped hanging around campus waiting for me. She doesn't like me. And why the hell would she? These days, I'm all the fun of a funeral.

I stare up at the ceiling as this obvious truth hits me. She gave me a chance. She gave me multiple chances until she finally realized I'm an antisocial outcast. Life is too short to waste time on people who don't lift you up, who don't inspire you—they'll eventually drain you. She's moved on to people who will make her laugh, make her feel like her presence is appreciated. All this time, I completely missed out on getting to know her.

I sink down in my seat. I am such a stupid asshole. She was different from any girl I've ever met, and I was too cynical and scared to act on it.

* * * * *

*After class I drive to Video Hutch for my work shift.* I pass Taco Boys to grab lunch, and there, in bold black letters on the sign outside are the words GRAY'S SPECIAL. HALF OFF QUESADILLAS! I pull into the parking lot and blink up at the sign with disbelief. I walk inside and instinctively pull my hat low over my head. I scan the room to make sure I don't recognize anyone. I saunter up to the counter and there, on the wall next to the cash registers for all to see, is every page of Dylan's ridiculous letter, framed like an award. Surrounded by hearts and rainbows in classy script, is my name: Gray Thomas.

I pick my jaw up off my chest and stand in line for my order. I duck my head low and listen as everyone in front of me asks for Gray's Special. When it's my turn, I tighten my lips and ask for two beef burritos and a side of nachos to go. The worker types in my order with a bored look and asks for my name. I hand her the cash and avoid her eyes.

"Mike," I say.

* * * * *

*I was counting on work to distract me.* I planned on playing a comedy. *Major League* or *The Jerk*. Maybe a slasher film would be a good distraction. *Saw III*. Or, I could go all-out depressing. *Schindler's List*. That film would make my problems seem minuscule. But when I clock in, my manger, Dillon (nice name, huh?), sticks me in the back to unload and label new movie arrivals as if he's trying to punish me, as if the local news announced to the entire city what a dipshit I am for passing up the most amazing woman in town. I sit in the storage space, the size of a closet, where my thoughts threaten to crush me.

After work I drive home, my mood close to depressed, and pull in next to my mom's car. My dad's out of town on another business trip. I haven't seen him in weeks. My mom usually works herself to exhaustion and comes home long enough to take a shower and pass out by eight p.m. She's a high school history teacher, and she used to take the summers off to golf, paint, and plan family road trips (usually of historical importance, to my boredom). Not anymore. This summer she's teaching two classes at the high school. Two more at a community college. Distractions, distractions.

There's a note for me on the kitchen table.

*It was a really long day! I'm beyond tired — dinner is in the fridge! I love you. Good night. — Mom*

I glance at the clock and push out a heavy sigh. It's only 8:23.

I sit on the couch in the basement and finish off leftover pizza. It's stale and lukewarm and the cheese is cemented to the dough. I don't care. I don't really taste it anyway. As I flip between ESPN and Comedy Central, I hear a knock at the front door. I walk upstairs, and when I open the door my stomach leaps as I see Dylan, smiling brilliantly, holding a bouquet of orange and purple flowers.

"Dylan!" I say, and almost grab her in my arms. I hold on to the door frame to keep myself from acting so overjoyed. I have to be somewhat cool.

She holds out the flowers. "They're for your mom," she says. She tells me they're birds of paradise, her favorite flower. I accept the bouquet but my eyes are fixed only on her. Her hair is loose and falls around her shoulders. She's wearing a baggy T-shirt and jeans with rips to expose both of her knobby knees. I wonder if she'll ever try to look feminine. I'm also starting to wonder what her body looks like underneath all her oversize clothes.

I realize my memory's parched, and I drink her in. Did I really mistake this gorgeous girl for being awkward? Staring at her now, she's the most confident person I've ever seen.

"I hope your neighbors won't mind I picked them out of their garden," she says as she breezes past me into the foyer. My eyes snap off of her body to examine the flowers.

"You picked these from next door?" I ask, my voice tense. I know very little about our retired neighbors, the Paulsons. But one thing I am aware of is that Mrs. Paulson is more protective of her desert garden than a mother bear is of newborn cubs.

Dylan grins and tells me she's kidding. She'd never be so mean. She follows me down the hall to the kitchen and I glare at her over my shoulder.

"Where have you been all week?" I demand, like I'm her boyfriend and she hasn't called to check in. She doesn't look bothered by the time that's lapsed since we've seen each other. She runs her fingers along the marble countertop and studies pictures on the refrigerator. She tells me she went to Tucson with her aunt for a few days to volunteer at an art festival.

"Did you miss me?" she asks, and leans close to me, her eyes fixed on mine. My eyes fall to her lips, curved in a small grin, like she's trying to be sexy. And it's really sexy. I clear my throat and turn away to look in the cupboard for a vase.

She asks, with a tone of disappointment, if I have a dog. I say no and her mouth falls a little.

"I didn't think so."

I set the flowers in a glass jar and she tells me she misses her dogs back home and needs a puppy fix.

"What made you come to Phoenix for the summer, exactly?" I finally ask.

She tells me she's always wanted to walk on her hands.

"What?" I ask.

"You know, break free from the norm. See life from a whole new perspective. Arizona is about as opposite from Wisconsin as you can get."

She says they don't have deserts in Wisconsin. They have humidity and thunderstorms and mosquitoes. They have lakes, huge lakes, and rivers and dark forests and fields full of fireflies.

"But no saguaros," she adds.

I raise my eyebrows because I think there's more to her decision than a change in landscape. "You drove thousands of miles from home to see a cactus?"

"No," she says. "I came out here to start my life."

"You weren't alive in Wisconsin?" I joke. "What, were you in a coma?"

She nods. "I was cryogenically frozen until two months ago."

"Right."

"I might as well have been," she says. She tells me she grew up in a small town where life was safe, but that was the problem. It was too known, too predictable. It's hard to feel adventurous when you know where every road leads. It's hard to be unique when everyone in high school is grouped together and pre-labeled, like a packaged brand.

I nod because I can relate. In high school so much of your life is already scheduled out for you, you barely feel like you're living it — more like you're assigned to it. Your future doesn't loom — it just sways lazily like an old familiar blanket drying on a clothesline in the sun. It isn't liberating; it's confining.

"If you never leave where you come from, I don't think you'll ever figure out who you are," she says. "Because how much is forced on you? How much of your personality is imposed instead of created? That's why I left. I think people need to leave in order to find their potential."

"Don't you miss your friends?" I ask.

She shakes her head and says she doesn't really miss people. "I'm always too excited imagining the people I'm about to meet. If you only focus on the things you leave behind, you'll never go anywhere."

I tell her maybe she's too good for that small town, but she shakes her head.

"I never felt *better* than anyone. Just misplaced. Like there's something more waiting for me. At the end of the day, I just want to be inspired. That's it."

She helps me arrange the flowers. When she's satisfied, she asks if we can give them to my mom.

"She's in bed," I say, and Dylan and I both turn to glance at the clock on the microwave. It isn't even nine. I look down at my feet and wait for the questions, for Dylan to judge my mom. Our lifestyle. Our quiet house. Our lifeless house. But she surprises me, as usual.

"Want to get out of here?" she asks, as if she can feel the weight of my thoughts. I wonder if she can, if she's starting to know me that well. I nod and she turns, taking long-legged strides toward the front door.

# ||| FIRST UNFOLD |||

## Dylan

*Pickle coughs to life and I turn up the volume* to Cat Stevens. As we drive, his weathered voice matches the cracked desert scenery. Gray sifts through my CD collection in the console between us. I ask him what he's doing and he informs me it's the ultimate friendship test.

"I need to approve of your music taste," he says, as if this is a pivotal moment in our relationship.

"That sounds a little judgmental," I say.

"I am judgmental," he points out. He explains that if you look at your good friends, you always have similar music tastes. It comes down to an issue of respect.

"Can someone who listens to Miley Cyrus really have a long-lasting relationship with an indie rock band connoisseur?" he asks.

"Sure," I say.

"Not a chance." He insists the kind of music you listen to says so much about your choices in life. The girl who listens to Miley Cyrus gets coffee at Starbucks, while the indie rock band connoisseur only buys local. She joins a sorority and he joins a garage band. She shops at boutiques and he will only set foot in thrift stores. She goes to Cancun for spring break. He skis in Boulder. Nothing in common.

"You have some very interesting theories, Gray," I say.

I only have a couple albums, and he's surprised my car actually has a working CD player. He flips through them and offers short critiques: Cat Stevens's greatest hits (excellent compilation), the Killers (great album), the Cure (impressive), Paul Simon (essential), and the Clash. He meets my eyes and smiles, and I see his respect for me skyrocket.

"So, where do you want to go?" I ask, secretly pleased I passed his test. I rarely care what people think of me, but with Gray, even a trace of a smile feels like a compliment because I know it's sincere. He couldn't be fake if he tried. He points straight ahead, to a small cluster of lights in the distance.

"Camelback Mountain," he says. I nod and turn the music up. We both look out at the fading light in the sky. The desert is world-famous for her sunsets. At night, she dresses up the sky with a shawl of feathery clouds. Her horizon is so vast, so sparse, that the skyline stretches for hundreds of miles and a neon color show highlights the world. Tonight her metallic pinks and oranges drape over the low, purple hills in the distance. The sight is spellbinding enough to make the devil admit there's beauty on earth.

We drive up the slope of Camelback and I pull off to the shoulder when mansions creep into view, built against the steep, rocky bluffs. We park and climb the road on foot to get a better look at the monstrous homes, spaced acres apart. Hot air presses against us as if it's blown in from a distant fire. We stop to stare up at a miniature castle complete with spindly towers and crenellated rooftops. We make up stories about the people who live inside. Gray predicts most of them are lawyers or doctors. I imagine they're full of scientists cloning endangered species, or kung fu fighters training CIA agents for hand-to-hand combat. Maybe engineers live inside, building a giant robot army to defend Earth from the coming alien attack from Mars. I claim one house is a fancy boarding school for celebrity children and another, a rehab clinic for the celebrity children's parents.

We stop walking when we stumble onto an empty lot, where a house is beginning construction. The ground has been leveled and a cement foundation was recently poured. We walk around the cement ground and design the house. We put the bathroom in the corner, the kitchen facing northwest. I map out the living room, where the fireplace will go and how the wing chairs will be situated. Gray informs me the room needs a sectional, or at a minimum, two recliners.

"You can't watch sports in wing-backed chairs," he argues. I inform him there will be no television in this house, which starts a heated debate, only resolved by a compromise. There will be a television in the basement. And surround-sound speakers. And a poker table.

We decide it needs a second story for bedrooms and a loft because lofts are perfect for building forts, a necessity in any sensible home design. I point out the dining room would work best coming off the back end of the house, where the view of the city is a galaxy of lights, hundreds of feet below.

We sit down at the edge of the foundation, both of us visualizing our finished house. I ask Gray if he could live anywhere, where it would be.

He leans back on his hands.

"I'd live in New Zealand," he says, "on the North Island." He tells me his dad collects travel photography books piled on the living room table and that's where he discovered the spot. In the tip of New Zealand, the island breaks off into tiny clusters, and those make up the Bay of Islands. He'd live in the middle of them, in a white beach house with huge windows looking out at the sea. He'd sleep outside on the porch every night. He'd own kayaks and speedboats and go parasailing every day. He'd learn how to sail.

I watch his face change as he talks. It becomes more hopeful, as if he's looking into the future for the first time and imagining it could be a paradise. It's a new attitude for him.

## Gray

*I'm trying to concentrate on the city skyline below,* but my eyes keep getting pulled down to the rip in Dylan's jeans, exposing her naked knee. I'm tempted to run my hand over her skin, and the ache to touch her becomes so powerful, my fingers start to burn.

"Can I ask you something?" I say. I hesitantly pick up my hand and run it through her hair. It falls soft between each of my fingers. My heart races from the touch. Dylan inhales a sharp breath and meets my eyes. Bits of light reflect inside them.

"Why are you here?" I ask. She stares at me with surprise. I drop my hand out of her hair so I can think clearly. "I'm not stupid," I say. "I know I'm not a party to be around. I'm cynical and boring and I'm not even nice to you."

"You're not boring," she insists. "And you can be nice. I think it's accidental, but it does happen."

"You know what I mean," I say. We both have our sandals off and I run my toe along the top of her foot, down to her bony ankle. She doesn't move it away. "I've spent half the time trying to blow you off. Which I feel really bad about, by the way. And I'm glad you came back. But why did you?"

She smiles.

"And don't say it's because I'm cute," I add.

She shrugs. "I don't know. You're a challenge," she says. I raise my eyebrows at this simple answer and tell her I'm sure she can find more upbeat, happy people in this city that are also a challenge.

"But they wouldn't have your prolific theories," she points out. Well, that is true.

"I like people that take time to figure out," she says. "That's one thing I'll never be—mysterious. I put it all out there. So, I'm intrigued by people who make it hard to get to know them. People opposite me, I guess."

She studies my confused expression. "You play video games, right?" she asks. I nod. What guy doesn't?

"Okay, you know how in video games, the character you're trying to beat has a life bar at the bottom of the screen that you need to break down? But you need to learn all their moves and defenses before you can? Well, you're kind of like that."

I look away as I visualize this random analogy. "So, you're trying to deplete my life bar?"

She smirks as she applies some Chap Stick to her lips.

I'm jealous of Chap Stick. There's a first.

"I'm trying to kick down all these walls you've built up to see what's underneath. The more I knock them down, the more I like what I see," she says. "And I think you're cute," she adds.

She looks out at the lights below and changes the subject.

"You know what I love most about the desert?" she asks. I shake my head. "It's the only place where the earth is stripped naked. Totally exposed. It's like you can't help but be yourself when you're surrounded by it. You can't help but bare your thoughts."

She looks back at me and waits. Her eyes are determined.

"Okay," I say. I ask her what she wants to know.

"Why all the walls, Gray?" she asks. "What's going on with you?" I turn my body away from her and stare out at the bowl of lights below our dangling feet. I could play dumb. I could lie. But I don't want to. Not with her.

I look back at Dylan. I have to confess to someone. It's cracking inside me.

"My family's falling apart," I finally say. Dylan's eyes turn into their listening mode, where they focus on mine and invite me to come inside and stay awhile. I inhale a long breath. I'm not sure I'm prepared to open up this conversation. My hands clench into fists.

"What happened?" she asks.

"My mom's depressed," I say. "My dad's never home. When he is, it's like he's sleepwalking. We haven't spoken in months." Dylan's silent next to me. I look over at her with hard eyes. "I'm not asking you to feel sorry for me. It's just what we're going through."

She nods and I take another deep breath. I tell her the truth. I tell her my sister died, my twin sister, about eight months ago, and my mind and heart twist with anger at hearing the words out loud. I thought the pain would get easier, but it always stings, like a snakebite, through my core, down to my bones. I still haven't accepted her death. It's easier to imagine she's just away on a long trip. Traveling the world. That she'll show up any day and surprise us.

"It hasn't been good," I say, and pull down the rim of my hat.

I tell Dylan she died in a car accident. She hit black ice on the way to Flagstaff in a snowstorm and spun out of control. It ripped my family apart, and now I'm the only thing holding us together. I'm the glue, and it's a weak hold at best.

"You don't want to be here," Dylan says. She doesn't ask. She knows. She can see it in my eyes.

"No. Everything here reminds me of her. It's like I'm living in a graveyard."

"What's her name?"

"Amanda."

"And you two were really close?" she asks.

"Yeah. She dated one of my best friends in high school for a while—Brandon, the guy you met on Mill Avenue. We hung out all the time." Most guys would never admit being best friends with their sister, but I tell Dylan she was like a soul mate.

"I don't remember the month after her death." I smile to myself. "I think I went to the dark side for a while."

"Did you miss any school?"

I shake my head and tell her school was the only thing that got me through it. But it's like I was in a coma the whole time. Six months of my life was a blur. I didn't play baseball—I couldn't. My mind was too numb. I ignored all my friends; they just reminded me of her. Then they all graduated and moved on with their lives. The ones that stuck around called for a while, but they eventually stopped.

"And you feel like you need to stay in Phoenix to be close to your parents?"

I nod.

"Were you planning on going to school?"

I tell her I had a scholarship offer to play baseball in New Mexico, before Amanda died. I gave it up to stay home. There's no way I could pack up my life and leave my parents alone.

"I bet your sister would have wanted you to play," she says.

She's right. Amanda would be furious with me. She'd kick my ass to New Mexico. I can imagine her in heaven, complaining about how I'm wasting my life away, and trying to persuade angels to fly down and smack me in the head with their halos until I come to my senses.

"And your mom isn't coping very well?"

I shake my head and tell her she still cries every day. I can hear her at night. But she doesn't want to talk about it. We don't even say Amanda's name in the house. It just hangs in the air like smoke that hasn't settled yet.

Dylan asks me all kinds of questions about my sister. What was she like, did she play sports, what her hobbies were. It feels good to talk about Amanda, to lift up the shade of memories. It lets some light in.

We sit in our imaginary dining room for hours, and it's starting to feel like home. I finally stand up and pull Dylan up next to me. We walk in silence back to her car. As we drive home, all my thoughts filter back to Amanda and the night the police called about the accident. I think about the drive, the longest drive of my life, up to the hospital in Flagstaff where my sister was dying in an intensive care unit. And I always wonder what was going through her head. I wonder if she was scared or in pain or even capable of thought. I wonder what you think about right before you end.

We never got to say goodbye. And a piece of me died with her that day.

Dylan turns down the radio and glances at me.

"Tomorrow's Saturday," she says in a voice that's always energized. I wait for it.

"I have an idea," she says.

"Of course you do," I say.

"Let's celebrate your sister tomorrow. Take me to all her favorite places. Where she hung out, where she went shopping, where she went out to eat. Let's honor her for the day. I want to see photos, I want to hear stories. What do you think?"

I stare back at her. "Why?"

"Because you loved her. And you need to spread her legacy."

I look out the window and consider this. I spent the last eight months avoiding the streets I drove down with my sister. Avoiding the people and places that made all the memories come back in nauseating waves.

"You don't have to do that."

"I want to. Starting tomorrow morning. Where should we go for breakfast?"

I smile at the memory.

"Tommy's. It's in Mesa," I say. "It's a dive, but the food is unbelievable. Best biscuits and gravy in the city."

"I'll pick you up at eight."

"Eight in the morning?"

She ignores my concern with sleeping in. "We have a lot of ground to cover. Start making a list."

When she drops me off, I get out of the car and my head feels lighter. For the first time in years, I feel like there's life after death.

* * * * *

*I'm trying to sleep,* but too many thoughts are spilling over my mind. I want to catch them and coax them to sleep so I can sleep, but they're determined to make me think. And I'm thinking about one girl in particular.

What the hell is happening between me and Dylan? Everything is backwards with this girl. Call me close-minded, but usually dates don't involve celebrating the life of a dead relative. It doesn't exactly set the mood for romance. Then again, is this even a date?

I'm not a licensed relationship expert, but in my experience when you're interested in someone things progress in predictable (and usually painful) phases: You check her out and catch her checking you out. You picture her naked, while she likes to refer to the mutual sexual attraction as "chemistry." Now it's time for the personality profiling. You make small talk between classes or after school or at work. You attempt to show subtle interest without being too obvious—it's all about maintaining mysterious indifference. If you come on too strong you're labeled as desperate, or a stalker. Overeagerness is up there with serial killer status as a way to fend off possible love interest. It's a careful balance, like a tightrope you need to cross over those first few weeks.

You play it safe. Send witty text messages. Make sure you've downloaded your best pictures online: you rock climbing (your adventurous, athletic side), playing Scrabble with Grandma (your easygoing, sensitive side), a group shot of you and your friends (Mr. Popular). There's only one conclusion to draw from this digital slideshow: You're a Catch. Once that definitive answer is reached, eventually, you hang out in person and let your oddball shine through. And this is usually when things go bad, or like Amanda and I used to say, when the cheese gets old and moldy.

What I don't think is normal is anything that defines my relationship with Dylan. I still don't even have her phone number. Tonight I spent half the time thinking about kissing her. Wondering how she'd react. Wondering when I should try.

I can't even figure out if she wants me to kiss her. She holds my hand and calls me cute, but girls hold each other's hands and call each other cute (kind of a turn-on, actually), so what am I? What if she just sees me as a brother type? God, no, please. What if she ropes me into her random plans because she wants a buddy? A sidekick? She doesn't really flirt with me. She touches me, but she doesn't stare into my eyes like girls do when they want you to kiss them, with that dreamy, lovesick gaze.

I played the leaning game tonight. It's this stupid theory I've heard, that if she leans her legs or shoulders or head toward you, it's body language saying she likes you. But this girl doesn't sit still long enough to confirm anything other than she's hyper.

I'm at a critical point here where I could miss my opportunity and fall into the dreaded and irreversible Friend Zone, the ultimate dead end. Every guy's greatest fear and deepest remorse.

But how am I supposed to set the mood when Dylan could win an award for the most awkward dating ideas of all time?

# ||| First Trust |||

## Dylan

*I pull into his driveway at* 8:01 and before I turn off the engine the front door opens and Gray walks out in his usual T-shirt, shorts, and flip-flops. I stick my head out of the car window and frown.

"You're missing something," I inform him. He assumes I'm referring to the fact that he's hatless today. He shrugs and runs his hand through his hair, which, no matter how hard he attempts to control it, resembles something close to shag carpeting. It's one of his best features. I kill the engine and spring out of the car. He blinks heavily and informs me I have way too much energy this early in the morning.

"Where are the pictures?" I demand. He looks down at his empty hands.

"You were serious about that?" he asks. I press a stubborn hand against my hip to assure him I was.

I push his shoulder to steer him back toward the house. I follow him downstairs and he turns the hallway corner and flips on his bedroom light. He tells me after Amanda died, he packed away every photo he had of her and shoved them in his closet, where they've yet to be touched. He opens his closet and searches deep in the back for his box of memorabilia.

I look around his room. It smells clean, as if it's recently been vacuumed. His bed's in the corner and a dark blue comforter is kicked to the side. The pillows are tossed in disarray, and the sheets are untucked and balled up like he's a restless sleeper, or maybe he doesn't sleep at all. A few clothes litter the carpet. There are two guitars in one corner with stacks of CDs piled around them. A few sports jerseys and concert posters are tacked on the walls.

His bookshelf catches my eye because it isn't crammed with books — it's cluttered with rows of trophies, plaques, and medals. Gray walks over to me with a tinge of embarrassment.

"It's like my own personal shrine," he admits. We look at the shiny gold figurines perched on top of miniature wood and marble columns. Tiny heroes. Golden moments. There has to be a hundred of them. I read some of the awards, a few for MVP, some for batting, but most of them are for pitching.

"I didn't realize it meant so much to you," I say.

"Maybe it's time to pack them up," he says, his voice hard. "I need to move on from high school."

I know there's more to it than that. They're memories of his best times, his glory years. They're also a reminder of the dreams he's giving up.

"They don't make trophies for the right reasons," I say. I tell him they should award people for owning the greatest sock collection, or giving the best hugs, or being the nicest guy. Gray frowns and informs me no guy would ever want to win an award for being nice.

He sets a brown shoe box down on the bed and I pull off the lid. I wince at the picture sitting on top. It's a black-and-white headshot of Amanda, with a piece of yarn threaded through a hole punched at the top. He tells me his cousins wore her picture around their neck at her funeral. Amanda looks a lot like Gray, same dark hair, but hers was straight and long. Same wide, entrancing smile.

It's hard for me to look at her eyes. There's so much life inside them. I pick up a second picture of Amanda with a piece of yarn threaded through it and hand it to Gray.

"These are perfect," I say, and pull the yarn over my head. He stares down at the picture and his eyes fog over for a second. I place a photo around his neck before he can argue, and he sighs like he can't believe he's going through with this. He grabs an envelope of pictures from the box and I take his free hand.

*\* \* \* \* \**

*We begin the journey at Tommy's Café* and order their famous biscuits and gravy. We each offer Amanda a bite. Neither of us is a huge coffee drinker, but Amanda was, so in her honor we both slam two cups of liquid crack. Gray's so jittery, he can't stop his feet from tapping, and I attempt to play the drum solo of "Wipeout" on the table with my silverware until the waitstaff's annoyed stares give us the hint that we're completely obnoxious.

I sit in the booth next to Gray and he walks me through every photo. He shows me pictures from Christmas, when they used to have huge family get-togethers and everyone had to write and perform an original play. He shows me the picture of the winning year—when he, Amanda, and their two cousins wrote the dark comedy "Pulp Christmas," about a drug-induced family holiday. We look at photos of a garage band he started with his sister—he was on guitar, she was lead vocals and tambourine, and his neighbors were bongo and bass. They called themselves Lucky Dogs and played mostly Adam Sandler covers, Bohemian-style.

Gray tells me one of his favorite stories. During their sophomore year of high school, Amanda went a day without using her arms. When Gray asked her why she was doing it, she said because it "puts life in perspective." He told her she was being ridiculous. Why would you want to experience having a severe birth defect? She argued you could lose your arms any day. It makes you appreciate what you have.

So, his mom helped her get dressed and brush her teeth. He fed her breakfast, drove her to school, and hauled her bags to her locker. Her friends fed her lunch and carried her books to class. She got out of doing all her homework. Not fair.

She went to track practice after school and ran with the team, but she kept her arms tucked close to her sides. That's the picture he's holding as he's telling me this story—a photo of Amanda running around the track with her arms held tight against her hips. People stared at her, he said, but she was too busy sprinting past them to notice.

"I don't even want to know how she went to the bathroom," Gray added. "I never asked."

She wrote an essay about her experience and published it in their school paper. It won an award for the most creative essay that year. People still talk about it. I tell him I'd love to read it.

We leave Tommy's and drive out to Scottsdale to visit an art gallery where Amanda worked part-time. We walk in and he points out a piece she made that still hangs in the store, in memory of her. It's a mosaic. Amanda always found beauty in the most random things, he explains.

"You two have that in common." He tells me she collected rocks, glass, or anything chipped and tattered that most people overlook. Where most people saw trash, Amanda saw potential and she could somehow string broken pieces together to create something beautiful. He says she sold one of her pieces, when she was fifteen, for four hundred dollars.

"Amanda wanted to go into art therapy," he explains. "She

wanted to work with people with disabilities and open her own art studio. She would have been great at it."

I smile sadly at the idea of her. It's hard to accept that you've missed out on a *person*, that all you'll ever know of them are pieced-together stories. It's not like missing out on a party or a concert—those are temporary experiences, and you'll have other opportunities. But this is permanent. It's like being robbed of something valuable you never had the privilege to own.

"I wish I could have known her" is all I can say.

"You would have loved her," he says. "It's scary how well you two would have gotten along."

We walk across the street to Nella's Irish Bar and Restaurant and I follow Gray to the back, where there's a Ms. Pac-Man video game, one of his and Amanda's favorite and most addictive pastimes. He lays a stack of quarters on the table next to the game and crosses his arms over his chest.

"Another quintessential test of any friendship," he says, and nods at the screen. "Do you appreciate old school video games?" Instead of answering him, I grab a handful of quarters. It just so happens that I not only appreciate Ms. Pac-Man, but share his obsession. By the time we leave, I have a blister forming on the back of my thumb from playing so long. Gray has to pull me away from the machine when I almost dislocate my shoulder from taking a hard right to escape a ghost. When I make it to level two, he's impressed. When I make it to level four, he just gawks.

"Okay, I'm seriously turned on," he says with a smile, and I can feel myself blush.

We head down the street and walk into the Coffee Bean and Tea Leaf, where Amanda stopped every day for a Vanilla Ice Blended. We each order one and drive out to today's most sacred destination spot: the Tracks. Gray makes me swear on Pickle's life that I'll keep its location a secret.

We pass a warehouse district, and when the road dead ends there's a rough gravel path, camouflaged inside a sandy field. You wouldn't know it's there unless you were looking for it. The gravel road loops around the back of an old concrete factory. We drive down the path, Pickle bouncing angrily underneath us, until we reach the bottom legs of a shallow bridge, built to allow railroad tracks to pass under the city streets. Gray says this is where he spent most of his weekends in high school. I don't need him to explain why he'd want to hang out under a bridge next to railroad tracks. I get it. It's an escape. Too much one-on-one time with reality is the fast track to despair. I open up the car door before he has a chance to say "We're here."

We crawl up the steep concrete slope to a shaded ledge carved out where the support beams meet the road above. We sit down, perched high off the ground, and look out at the dusty railroad tracks below. Cars speed by overhead to remind us that life keeps moving. But under this dark shelter it's easy to hold the world over your head so no one can watch you, no one can judge you. No one can say you're doing it wrong.

Gray tells me Amanda discovered this spot. It's invisible from the street above, blocked by the warehouse buildings. This makes it completely private, open to only a few worthy patrons. This is where he came on the weekends with friends. For a brief period of time on a Friday or Saturday night, they called the shots, and no one could bring them down. Life was theirs to control, not structured and mandated by parents and teachers, coaches and schedules.

He says after Amanda died, he skipped class sometimes to come out here by himself and smoke.

"I didn't even like smoking," he says. "But I needed something to force me to breathe. Sometimes it took effort just to breathe."

"No one else comes out here?" I ask.

"After she died it became a memorial. I still find letters left for Amanda, from the few people that know this place exists. People leave photographs and flowers. Once in a while they leave letters for me."

We're quiet for a few minutes. The only sounds are cars speeding by overhead. But they feel distant, like memories, like we're worlds away from everyone.

"Amanda was cremated," Gray says, his tone almost emotionless. We look out at the dusty tracks below us. The sun is blinding bright.

"This is her tombstone to me," he says.

* * * * *

*We grab a late lunch at a café* his sister loved called Gecko Grub in Tempe. We sit at the outdoor patio, where Amanda used to spend hours people watching. We order burgers and curly fries and milk shakes.

"Amanda had excellent taste," I say as I pop a fry into my mouth. I haven't spoken very much today. I only ask questions. I listen. Learning about Amanda is like getting to know another side of Gray — his adventurous, ridiculous side. His happiest side. People become pieces inside of you. They can fill you up and make you whole. I think Amanda is his favorite piece, the one he is most proud of. Now I can understand why he caved in.

"How do you feel about all this?" I ask.

Gray picks at his fries. "I wouldn't call today fun," he admits. "But it wasn't awful either. I didn't know what to expect."

I nod slowly and wait for him to continue. He looks up at me and realizes there's more to my question. He sits back in his chair and looks out at the street. Today was all about the past. It was about bringing Amanda back to life. But it's time to come back to reality.

Gray speaks slowly, like he's trying to hold himself together.

"I'm just trying to figure out how to live without her," he says. "That's the hardest part. I know you'll never meet her. I know she won't get married or go to school or have a family—all the things she deserved to experience. I just can't accept that she's only a memory now. She deserves so much more than that."

We're both quiet for a few seconds. I feel my forehead crease, and start fidgeting with my napkin. Gray's watching me.

"What is it?" he asks.

"I don't know what to say," I admit. "I hate that. I wish I had all the answers for you. I wish I could explain why this happened."

He shakes his head. "Don't. Don't say anything. I'd rather you say nothing than say something stupid, like 'Oh, now she's in heaven, where she belongs because she was too perfect to live on earth.' I hate it when people say that."

He exhales sharply and I can see the anger filling his eyes.

"I mean, there's no one like her. No one. She touched every person's life that was lucky enough to know her. Everyone loved her. Of all the stupid, selfish, people that get to live, every day, she had to die. Why? Because she's an angel and she belongs in heaven?"

I shake my head.

"Well, fuck heaven," he says. His eyes start to water but he's too angry to care. "We need people like Amanda here, on earth. Because there aren't enough good people left. Heaven can wait."

Gray sucks in a deep breath to try to calm down. He's waited too long to talk about Amanda. To open up his memories. He wasn't doing Amanda any honor by letting himself shrivel up and drown in anger and denial and depression. Now I know why his face looked so blank when we first met, why his eyes were so vacant all the time. He wasn't even living. He was just hiding away to avoid the pain.

But pain's like water. It finds a way to push through any seal. There's no way to stop it. Sometimes you have to let yourself sink inside of it before you can learn how to swim to the surface.

* * * * *

*Our last stop is one of Amanda's favorite music stores,* Happy Trail Records. It has a mix of new and used music, but it's best known for its selection of vintage concert T-shirts and posters in the back of the store.

While Gray's looking through CDs, I tell him we should do something for his mom.

"Like what?" he asks.

"Let's surprise her," I say. "Want to make her dinner?"

His mouth twitches like he's trying to fight a smile. "Do you cook?" he asks.

"I prepare an amazing frozen pizza," I offer.

"Wow," he says. "I heard preheating an oven is an acquired skill."

I nod. "What's your specialty?"

He leans against the CD rack and admits his own culinary expertise involves microwaving leftovers. "And I make exceptional turkey sandwiches," he adds. "The bread to turkey to mayo ratio is tricky, but I've mastered it."

"Okay, scratch dinner plans," I say. "We can get her a card. What about chocolate? Does she like chocolate?"

He stares at me. "What woman doesn't?"

"True, that's not very original. What else does she like?"

"Sleeping," he says. I wait until he gives me something to

work with. "All right—my dad used to surprise her with a bottle of wine. That always made her day."

"Red or white?"

"Red. I think she likes Shiraz or something."

We walk out to my car and I wonder out loud how we can get her a bottle, and Gray smiles.

"Maybe we should settle for chocolate," he says.

# ||| FIRST KISS |||

## Gray

*We drive back to Dylan's aunt's house* and I follow her inside. The interior is as immaculate as the outdoor landscape. It looks like an art museum, cluttered with statues, paintings, and sculptures. Dylan walks me around the living room and introduces me to plants she named: Ivo, Ivy, Ivan, and Yvette. She points out her red backpack on the floor is Ruby.

"You have a naming fetish," I inform her.

She tells me she names everything. Even her freckles. She turns her arm over and introduces me to two freckles close to each other on her forearm, Blake and Stacey. She claims they got in a fight with a third freckle, Meredith, farther up her arm near her elbow. I don't encourage the conversation any further.

We slump down on the leather couch and contemplate what to get my mom. Well, she contemplates what to get my mom. I contemplate kissing her. I strategically sat down close enough that our arms are touching. My calf brushes against hers. It makes my entire leg heat up.

Now. Do it now, you chump. Kiss her.

My eyes slip down to her lips and then back to her eyes. It's a way of asking permission. But she's oblivious. She's not even looking at me.

"I want to get her some wine," she says with a determined nod. I sigh, because we are on such completely opposite missions right now. I pull my fingers through my hair.

"Why do you want to get her the one thing we can't buy?"

"Because she'll never suspect it's from us. It will be a completely random surprise, and those are the best kind."

I look around the room. "Does your Aunt Dan have any wine?" I ask. We head to the kitchen and search her aunt's refrigerator and pantry with no luck.

Dylan paces back and forth in front of the counter. "We could steal it."

"That's a phenomenal idea," I say.

She stops pacing and looks at me. "Really?" she asks.

"Sure. Getting arrested would be the perfect surprise for my mom. I think it would really raise her sprits to think her last living child is a closet alcoholic with a criminal record."

"Good point. Well, then we need a pawn," she decides.

"A pawn?"

"Somebody to do the work for us. Do you know anybody who's twenty-one?"

I raise my shoulder and tell Dylan it would be a little rude to call friends I haven't spoken to all year just to ask them to go on a booze run for me.

"Then there's only one other option."

I look back at her plotting eyes. Uh-oh.

"What's that?" I ask.

\* \* \* \* \*

*Twenty minutes later I'm sitting* on Dylan's aunt's king-size bed while Dylan changes in the most gigantic walk-in closet I've ever seen. I glance around the bedroom, the size of an entire floor of my house. Everything in the room is decorated in blue and gold colors. Even the carpeting has flecks of sparkling gold in it. I wonder what man would ever willingly allow this kind of carpeting in his house. Maybe her husband was gay too, I decide.

"Where is your aunt, anyway?" I yell.

"She's in Vegas for a few weeks," Dylan shouts back through the closed door. "Don't worry, she wouldn't care if she came home. She's pretty laid back."

Dylan opens the closet door and walks out with a silly, lopsided grin on her face. I stare at her and bust up laughing. She managed to find a denim jumper. It looks like it was designed in the early eighties and it's short on her, falling at midcalf to expose her scrawny ankles. She's wearing a white turtleneck underneath it. The jumper balloons out around her, actually making Dylan look frumpy. She found some brown stockings with little pink cats on them, and she's wearing brown leather sandals with bows on the top. A beige leather purse with a braided strap hangs off her shoulder. She looks forty.

"Unbelievable," I say.

Dylan grins and turns to view herself in the full-length mirror. She hops up and down and claps her hands. Next comes the hair and makeup, she informs me. I follow her into the bathroom and we search through the drawers until we find an old basket of cosmetics. I watch Dylan apply bright red lipstick to her mouth, smudging some on her teeth, on purpose, and coating the outside of her lips too.

"This is what the tacky old ladies in Scottsdale do," she points out. She dusts her cheekbones with dark pink blush and adds a few moles to her skin with a black eyeliner pencil. She pulls half of her hair up in a barrette and finds some pearl earrings. It's beyond professional. And hilarious. And adorable. I think I love this girl.

Dylan sticks maxi pads on her shoulders underneath the

turtleneck (to my nauseating observation) to give her temporary shoulder pads. She also stuffs socks in her bra to give her "mommy boobs." I shake my head with admiration.

"It's go big or go home," she tells me. *Or get caught and go to jail,* I want to add.

She finds an old pair of tortoiseshell sunglasses and puts them on.

"What do you think?" She turns to face me, and I feel like I'm looking at my Aunt Mildred.

"You need a frump," I suggest.

"A what?"

"A front gut," I say, and pull a hand towel off the ring. I hand it to Dylan and tell her to stick it in her underpants. She gives me a questioning look and shoves the towel under her dress. We both crack up at the sight.

"I look pregnant," she says as she checks out her curves from the side.

"Yeah, maybe it doesn't work."

✳ ✳ ✳ ✳ ✳

*We drive downtown to the only grocery store* where I think we have a chance to pull this off. It's an Asian food market and a popular spot for underagers to test out their newly acquired fake IDs. I park the car at the side of the store where no one can see us from the entryway and Dylan lifts down the visor to use the small mirror. She puts on a fresh coat of lipstick and smacks her lips together.

"Just admit it," she says, and gives me a sideways glance. "How bad do you want me right now?"

I sigh like it's absolute torture to be sitting next to her. "Denim jumpers get me so hot," I say.

She opens the car door and shuffles toward the entrance. A minute later, I walk in after her. I can't pass up seeing this performance firsthand. The market's small—not much larger than a convenience store. Dylan wanders through the aisles, whistling, and stops occasionally and picks something up to pretend she's shopping. She swings her giant grandma purse and casually saunters over to a small selection of wine.

I watch Dylan approach the checkout counter out of the corner of my eye. I grab a pack of gum and get in line behind her. An Asian woman behind the counter scans her items. I look away and it takes every ounce of discipline I have to keep a straight face. Dylan's buying a can of tuna, a carton of eggs, and a bottle of red wine.

She flips through an *Enquirer* magazine and greets the cashier with a loud hello. Leave it to Dylan to strike up small talk while she attempts to break the law. I have to admit, she's fallen into character.

"My husband's watching the game with the boys tonight, so I finally get some alone time. And I'm celebrating!" Dylan says as she points at the wine.

The cashier chuckles and nods. They both laugh, apparently sharing a moment only two older domesticated women can appreciate.

I bite my lips together, waiting for some slip-up. But before I know it the cashier is asking me for sixty-five cents and Dylan's out the front door. I hand the woman my change and meet Dylan in the car. She has a calm look on her face while she adjusts the socks in her chest.

I sit down in the car and stare at her like she's some kind of superhero who just released her powers.

She takes her sunglasses off and smiles, her lipstick wet and shiny. Why do I find her hot right now? That's just wrong.

"It was almost too easy," she says.

I start the car and we pull away. "Tuna, eggs, and wine?" I say. "I think that's the most random purchase in Asian food store history."

Dylan shrugs. "I don't know," she says. "I wanted to be inconspicuous. I thought it would look weird if I just bought alcohol, so I tried to imagine what else a forty-year-old would buy."

I shake my head and tell her its genius. Dylan signs a card to my mom that we picked out earlier that day in Scottsdale. We agree to leave the card and bottle on our doorstep. I pull up to my house, knowing it's too early for my mom to be home, and Dylan glances around to make sure no one's looking (not that anyone would ever recognize her). She quickly sets the wine down on the front steps and sprints back to the car all hunched over like she's trying to duck under shotgun bullets.

A woman sprinting in a denim jumper. You don't see that every day.

"Okay," she says as she shuts the car door. "I seriously need to get out of this." She yanks on the tight collar of her turtleneck. I nod and silently agree she needs to get out of it. I want to offer to help.

We drive back to Dylan's house and she changes into a pair of sweatpants and a tank top. She spends almost a half hour in the bathroom, trying to scrub off her makeup. I lie on her aunt's bed and watch television, thinking about the day, coming down off a bittersweet high. I yell out, asking Dylan how she's doing. She yells back that the makeup won't come off. I get up and tap the bathroom door open to find Dylan standing there, frowning at her reflection in the mirror. The costume's gone and there's this beautiful girl standing in front of me. Her freckles are there again, her golden eyes. I can't take my eyes off of her. I can barely swallow. She sulks, blind to my buckling knees.

"I know," she says, and stares at her lips. "They're still pink."

I take a step toward her and reach out to take the warm, damp washcloth from her hand. It has smears of makeup all over it. I stare down at her soft lips, puffy from all the scrubbing, and hesitantly run my thumb across them. I feel Dylan shudder when I touch her. Or maybe it's me. I hold her face in my hand and look in her eyes and she offers me the smallest grin, and that's all I need. My eyes fall back to her lips. They look warm and soft and inviting.

My heart's pounding.

I close my eyes and lean down and press my lips against hers. For how skinny Dylan is, for how lanky and strange and goofy and hyper, kissing her is a totally different experience. She slows down. But it makes my insides speed up. Her mouth is smooth and sweet and confident.

She takes her time. It makes me crave more.

She opens her lips and touches my mouth with her tongue and it invites so many feelings to pour out of my mind and pump through my veins until my chest burns with something I've never felt before.

Love?

Whatever it is, it's real and it's terrifying and mystifying and even though my eyes are closed I can see showers of light.

I wrap my arms around Dylan and melt against her and I swear to God I could kiss this girl forever.

* * * * *

*Tonight, one relentless question invades my mind:* When can I kiss her again? It's all my brain cells want to focus on: That Kiss. That Kiss should be a new Hallmark holiday. A celebrated annual event. It was that good. I want to know what she thought of it. I don't need a play-by-play review. But That Kiss ended too soon and left me wanting more. And more and more.

I want to do something special for Dylan. I could buy her a gift, but I know she doesn't want material things. She doesn't wear nice jewelry. And I don't buy flowers. That's one gift I refuse to spend money on. I'm not going to hand over hard-earned cash for something that dies in a week.

I could take her out to dinner. Maybe to one of those trendy fusion restaurants (what that word means exactly is a mystery to me, since *fusion* just sounds like a combination of the words *futon* and *cushion*, nothing to do with food, so what am I missing?). But I doubt Dylan owns the right clothes for a fancy restaurant.

So, how do I surprise someone like Dylan? Get her a pet gecko? No, she'd just set it free after an awkward photo shoot.

Then, when I least expect it, inspiration strikes.

# ꓲꓲꓲ First Surprise ꓲꓲꓲ

## Dylan

*Gray picks me up after class,* and when I get in the car he announces he has a surprise. There's someone he wants me to meet—that's his only hint. After twenty minutes of failed attempts to pry any details out of him, we pull into a long strip mall parking lot. As soon as I see the sign for the Humane Society, I scream and open the car door before we've come to a complete stop. I jump out of the seat and race for the front doors, but Gray catches me in mid-sprint and holds me back.

"Wait," he says. "It's not what you think." I squirm to get out of his grasp and squint up at him.

"What do you *mean?*" It's the first time he's ever heard me whine, and it makes him laugh.

"I'm not getting a dog," he says. "My parents would kill me."

I frown and look between him and the entrance.

"But—"

"We're just renting one for the day," he warns me. "That's it. So try not to get too attached." We both know that's impossible.

I grab his hand and pull him toward the building because we're wasting time. A woman sitting behind the front counter greets us when we walk in, and Gray gives her his name.

"Oh, that's right," she says with a nod. "You're here for Boba." Gray explains to me that when he called earlier, he specifically said he didn't want a little dog, or even a cute one. He wanted the dog that needed the most love. The underdog of the dogs.

"There's no doubt that's Boba," the receptionist says.

After Gray signs a few papers and shows them ID, Boba's brought out to us. The back door swings open and Boba shuffles drunkenly in, all two hundred pounds of him. His sloppy tongue swings out of his mouth, narrowly missing the white tiled floor. If dogs can smile, this one's beaming, his droopy gums exposed in a slimy grin. His breaths come out in winded snorts. Gray asked for a dog that needs love, but this one looks like he just got dragged off his deathbed.

"He's perfect," I announce.

"He's a rhinoceros," Gray says, and leans over to study him. He mumbles something about hoping his car will hold him.

I fall to my knees and spread out my arms to greet Boba like he's long-lost family. A string of drool slips from his mouth and pools on the tile.

I cup his basketball-size head in my hands. "He is kind of a rhino, isn't he? He's just one big cuddly bear," I say, and scratch his slimy chin.

I glance at Gray to see he's more than slightly grossed out. I wait for him to say, *Is there an option two?* But he knows it's my purpose in life to love everything. Especially the underdog.

I scoop up Boba's hairy chest in my arms and press my face against his head and squeeze. I swear he squeezes back. It's mutual love at first sight.

"Is something rotting?" Gray asks, and sniffs the air.

"That's Boba," the receptionist explains. "He has a skin condition. We've tried washing him, but it's just his natural odor."

"Oh," Gray says, although it sounds more like *ew.*

Boba licks every bare inch of skin on my arms, and when he runs out of arms he licks my T-shirt. The receptionist tells us they think he's part mastiff, part pit bull.

"And part chronic salivater," Gray observes. He watches Boba lick my face and I see him grimace.

"He's taken with you," the receptionist says to me.

"Yeah," Gray agrees. "It's so cute."

I smile up at Gray. This is the best surprise anyone has ever given me. And in that instant, it makes me love him. Not in a heart-soaring, life-altering kind of way. It's just real. Effortless. In the past few weeks, he's become my best friend.

We walk outside and Boba struggles to make it twenty feet to the car. He's panting and drooling and I stay next to his side and encourage his every step. I assure him what a good boy he is and I list all the places we're going to take him, like Paris and the Mall of America and Madagascar.

Gray shakes his head. "You will go down in history as the easiest girl to impress."

He opens the door, and with a boost from both of us, Boba is soon the third passenger.

"This dog is going to have a heart attack," Gray says as he starts the car. I don't argue this point. I turn sideways in the seat to keep an eye on Boba and murmur to him that he'll be fine. I squeeze his paw in my hand.

"At least he'll die in the open air," I say. "Not in one of those nasty holding pens."

Boba smells like a kennel, and soon the whole car reeks like dog. He whips his head back and forth. Drool flies and wads of thick spit stick to the car windows.

"Dude, Boba, not cool," Gray yells at him.

I scold Gray. "He can't help it," I say. I grab a napkin and wipe a long string of spit off the dashboard, and we both crack up.

"Nice distance, Boba," I say.

Suddenly a stench overtakes the car that's so nauseating, my lungs threaten to shut down. I cover my nose with my hand and look out the window.

"Ugh," I groan. "I think we're passing a sewage treatment plant."

Gray rolls down the windows. "That's not what it is," he says. "Holy hell, Boba. You've got some serious ass gas."

We're both gagging. And laughing. Gray's car could be taped off by the authorities as an inhalation hazard zone. We pull over to the first dog spa we can find, because if we can't fix this dog's digestive issues, the least we can do is give him a bath. He smells like it's been a few years.

We realize too late that Boba has a fear of climbing out of cars, so Gray lifts his blubbery mass out of the back seat and Boba thanks him by slobbering in his ear. We don't bother to leash him up. He's not going to waddle off anywhere.

# Gray

*An hour later we're sitting outside in the shade,* eating ice cream. We treat Boba to his own cone in celebration of his tremendous achievement—walking three blocks. His new shiny coat gave him a small boost of energy. But there's still one problem.

"Does this dog eat sulfur?" I ask, and wave my hand in the air to wave off another fart. I swear he has them set on a timer. Every five minutes there's an impressive gust.

"Is there anything we can do about it?" Dylan wonders.

"We could take him to NASA and see if they can bottle his gas for rocket fuel," I propose.

She nods and agrees it's probably powerful enough.

Dylan points out a used bookstore down the street, and we

walk over to browse a cart full of one-dollar books. Boba staggers along behind us. Dylan informs me we're each going to pick out a book for the other.

It's a simple request. I scan the titles and try to imagine what Dylan reads, comedy or drama or classics or . . . *How to Build Miniature Doll Houses.* That one might be random enough for her. I try to find a book on photography and then my eyes catch the perfect title. I grab it and walk inside to pay.

When I come out, I watch Boba so Dylan can go inside. After we've both made our purchases, we swap. I lean against the building and pull my book out of the bag. I wonder what novel it's going to be. Maybe she found some Kurt Vonnegut. Or Ray Bradbury. I turn it over and read the title out loud.

*"The History of the Mullet."*

"Essential reading," Dylan says. "That haircut's almost extinct."

I stare at her. "Not in Alabama," I say. "But it should be. It should be illegal."

Dylan opens her bag and pulls out a used copy of *The Giving Tree* by Shel Silverstein. I still can't believe I found it used. Why would anyone willingly get rid of that book? My sister gave it to me right before she died, I tell Dylan. It's my all-time favorite.

We both admire our small treasures. She wraps her hand around my arm and we head to the car. I look over at Dylan as we drive back to the Humane Society. She's flipping through her book.

"Did you know my life has improved about ninety-nine percent since I met you?" I tell her. And that's not an exaggeration.

"That's because you're finally getting the hang of it," she says, and I ask her what she means. "You're not taking yourself as seriously."

I think about this. "So, that's the secret to happiness? Don't take life seriously?" I ask.

"No," she says. "Take life seriously. That you have to do. Don't take *yourself* seriously, that's the key. Let it all go. Don't care for a second what people think of you. In fact, go out of your way to keep them guessing."

We drive past a neighborhood park, and Dylan yanks on my arm and asks me to pull over. I lift Boba out of the car again and he walks about ten feet, until he finds the first spot of shade and slumps down from the overexertion. I sit down next to him and scratch his ears while Dylan investigates the park. There's a cobblestone path that weaves around it, with a stone fountain in the middle. She studies the layout the way an artist examines a painting and then announces this would be a perfect shot for a movie ending.

"It looks like the end of a Tom Hanks/Meg Ryan film," she decides.

"Oh," I say, "you mean one of those original endings where they meet for the first time and realize they've known each other all along?"

Dylan stands next to the fountain and nods in agreement. "Let's act it out."

Boba rests his heavy head in my lap. "Right," I say.

She won't be discouraged. "We'll call it . . . *Christmas Cookies in July.*"

"Sounds compelling."

"Come on, let's do the end scene," she says, and stands next to the fountain.

No way. I stare back at Dylan, waiting with her arms crossed stubbornly over her chest. She's caught on that today's all about her, and now she's going to milk my generosity it for all it's worth.

I glance around to make sure the park is completely abandoned before I agree to this. I stand up and walk out on the stone path. I pretend to look around for someone.

"Brinkley?" I yell. "Brinkley?!"

I hear Dylan laugh and I stare at her like I'm surprised she's there.

"You've seen *You've Got Mail?*" she asks me, as if doubting my masculinity.

I narrow my eyes defensively. "My sister loved that movie. She made me watch it."

"Sure, sure, whatever," Dylan says. She stops laughing and clears her throat and goes back into character. She takes a hesitant step toward me and places a hand over her heart.

"I can't believe it's you," she says. I take a step toward her. I can't believe I'm doing this.

"Um, you look good, Meg," I say, which sounds totally lame, but I suck at improv.

She frowns with disappointment.

"You don't, Tom," she says. "You have weird neck fat and your hairline is a mess and your face is all puffy. You're aging badly."

I take offense to this. "Hey, I have two Oscars. And how much Botox have you had, Meg? Let's be honest. Your career's as frozen as your face muscles. You can only do two expressions now — happy, sad, happy, sad, that's all you've got."

Dylan exaggerates a sad expression and I try not to laugh. "You know, that's just like you. I knew I hated you, especially when you copied my bakery idea and sold Christmas cookies in July," she says.

I shake my head. "You don't own the rights to Christmas cookies. Besides, it isn't personal, it's business."

Dylan looks around my feet. "Where's Jonah?"

I fall out of character. "Huh?"

Dylan waves her hand in the air. "Oh, I guess you haven't seen *Sleepless in Seattle*."

Just when we're about to hit the heavy make-out scene (the only reason I'm actually going through with this), a couple with a stroller wanders into the park and interrupts us. They see us holding hands next to the fountain and the woman smiles. The guy looks embarrassed for me. I wonder how much of our rehearsal they've witnessed. But I honestly don't care. Maybe Dylan's judgment-proof shield is wearing off on me.

We wave at the couple and leave the park with Boba shuffling behind us.

I look over at Dylan while we drive away. "Will you stay here forever?" I ask.

She smiles but doesn't answer me, and suddenly her eyes turn sad because the answer is no. Reality starts to seep in and I remember that summer days never last long enough. Especially now.

* * * * *

*It's past midnight and I'm nowhere near tired.* I'm strumming my guitar in my bedroom. I've got some Wilco tabs set out on the stand in front of me. I'm struggling with plucking the chords because it's almost impossible to concentrate on anything but her.

I have this huge grin stuck on my face. I'm relieved no one can see me looking so stupid. Because I can't wipe it away. First I thought she was crazy. Now I'm crazy about her.

There's a knock at my bedroom window. I set my guitar down and I don't have to open up the blinds to know who it is. I walk out the sliding back door of our basement and my feet hit the dry, prickly grass. It's warm out, and the night air feels like an oven. Dylan's standing there under the light of the moon in shorts and a T-shirt and these really furry slippers. I'm not the only one who isn't tired.

I grin and walk up to her.

"Do you want my phone number?" I ask. I figure it's about time we exchange them.

Dylan shakes her head and tells me she hates talking on the phone. It's too impersonal.

*So you prefer old-fashioned stalking,* I want to say. I tell her she can knock on my window anytime she wants. I hope she makes it a habit.

Dylan looks shy. I've never seen her like this. She's usually dangerously confident. I ask her what's wrong. She looks down at the ground and fidgets with the drawstring of her shorts.

"I couldn't sleep," she confesses.

"Why not?" I ask.

She smiles at me. It's this sweet, innocent smile, and it makes my heart stammer.

"You didn't kiss me today," she says. "And I wanted you to."

Bells are ringing in my ears. She's standing there waiting for me to make a move. I consider apologizing for this inexcusable mistake, but instead I save time. I close the distance between us and lean down and press my lips against hers. She smells like soap and shampoo and fresh air. She wraps her arms around me. I lift her shirt up and touch her warm skin. Oh, my God, I swear it's velvet. Instinct takes over.

We stumble through the basement door and I manage to close it without taking my lips off hers. It's hard to walk backwards and kiss at the same time without knocking our heads together. She's tall but I'm taller, so I lift her up and carry her to my room. We fall down on the bed and she pulls at my shirt and I pull hers up over her head. The room is spinning.

I turn the light off and catch my trophies out of the corner of my eye and I think of all the awards I would give to her. Best Kisser. Best Lips. Best Everything.

# ⅠⅠⅠ FIRST LOVE ⅠⅠⅠ

## Dylan

*I tell Gray I love him at Tommy's Café.* I think it's only appropriate to pick the most random ambiance to express my feelings. It makes for a better surprise. After commenting on the diner décor and arguing over whether a chocolate chip–bacon omelet would be disgusting or delectable, I announce:

"I love you and fried eggs and you more."

Gray chokes on a mouthful of biscuits and gravy and has to slam a glass of water before he can speak. I pretend to ignore his choking reaction and continue to ramble on about school and classes and where I want to go to college or maybe not go to college at all, just travel for a while.

I start making a list of where I'd like to travel because I'm incapable of any inner dialogue. Gray needs me to backtrack, so he holds up his hand to cut me off.

"Wait, what did you just say?" he asks. We stare at each other for a few seconds, the word *love* volleying back and forth between us, like a mental tennis match.

He needs the confirmation. I decide to play dumb.

"About what?" I ask. I take a sip of orange juice and wait for him to be more specific, but he steps around the word as if he's on thin ice.

"What did you say before you were talking about college?" He gives me this impatient stare. He's acting as if I just hit him with the heaviest word in the human vocabulary. But *love* doesn't carry that much weight to me. I've told lots of guys I love them. If you feel it, you say it, you spread it out. Life's too short to let love go to waste.

"I was talking about how this diner has the strangest décor I've ever seen," I say, noting again how the rainforest paintings clash with the 1950s parlor style.

He waves his hand in the air with impatience. "I know, we agreed on that. What did you say after that?"

He sets his fork down as if he's afraid he'll choke again. His face is tensing up and his eyes ask, *Did you say you love me? Or did I imagine it?*

I need to put him out of his misery.

"Oh. I said I love you. Is that what you're referring to?" I ask, and give him my best poker face.

His mouth falls open and he only stares at me, like he wants to say something but the words are stuck. I don't force it. When Gray doesn't know what to say, he closes up. Unlike me, he'd rather be quiet and reserved any day than a babbling motormouth. It's one of his best qualities.

I take a bite of my eggs and a long drink of orange juice. When I realize the conversation is one-sided when it comes to expressing our feelings, I go back to discussing my travel plans. But I can tell Gray isn't listening. His eyes are wandering. There's a question lingering behind them.

*You love me?*

\* \* \* \* \*

# Gray

*"I scared you yesterday, didn't I?"* she asks.

Dylan's lying in my arms on a hammock in our backyard. My feet hit the ground and I kick the hammock back and forth, like a swing. She came over again tonight in her pajamas and furry slippers (which she named, of course). Sometimes she talks to her slippers like they're her pets, and sometimes her slippers have full conversations with each other. It's borderline insane, but I let it go.

Now I leave the back door open for her. I'm starting to like our sleepovers, even though it's hard to get a second of sleep with her in my bed.

I hold Dylan tight against my side and tell her she scares me every day, but in a good way.

"It's what I said at Tom-Tom's," she prompts. I gulp, one of those nervous gulps where your whole throat constricts like there's a knot inside it. I know what she's getting at. Those three words.

"That I love you?" she adds, like I need clarification. "Is it so scary to hear it?" she asks. I look at her eyes, reflecting slivers of moonlight. I still can't believe how easily she says it. Where does she get her confidence? Do they sell a prescription of this stuff that I'm unaware of? Can I get a bottle? Doesn't she understand this changes everything?

"It's scary to say it," I tell her.

She sits up straighter and looks at me. "I don't get it. It shouldn't be scary at all. Shouldn't it be, I don't know, uplifting news?"

"It's a big deal. How many people have you said it to?"

Dylan thinks this over. A few seconds go by. Then almost a minute. Have there been that many?

"I'm sure when I was little I said it more often. I told a couple guys in middle school. Maybe ten guys in high school. I tell my girlfriends all the time. I told a guy at a gas station the other day I loved him because he helped check Pickle's oil."

I stare at her with a frown. My bubble of self-absorbed assurance that Dylan loves me, only me, bursts in the air.

"You tell that many people you love them?"

She blinks at me. "Sure. Why not?"

"I don't know. I don't think you should just throw the word around unless you really mean it."

"But I do mean it," she says. I'm flabbergasted. And annoyed. I ask her how she can love me and a gas station attendant she's known for five minutes. I tell her she uses the word too lightly.

She looks away and ponders this.

"I guess there are different levels of love," she says. "There's friend love and family love and platonic love and romantic love. And the levels of romantic love are endless. There's all-consuming love and desperate love and tortured love and that love/hate kind of love—"

I cover her mouth with my hand and tell her I get it.

"I think you're only meant to love a few people," I say.

"Why?" she asks.

I don't know how to explain it. It's just the way it is. "Because that's the way it works."

"That doesn't make sense," she argues. "Why limit it? Love is the one thing you can give away for free."

"It isn't free. People need to earn it."

"That's so sad to me," she says, "to think I can only use it on a select handful of people. Why can't we love everyone?"

"Because people are pricks," I say. I brush a piece of hair away from her face and tuck it behind her ear. I try to kiss her but she leans away and stares at me.

"You know what it is? We're taught to limit love. When you're a kid, you can say it to strangers. And then all of a sudden, one day you're reprimanded for it. The older we get, the closer we guard ourselves and the more selfish we are with giving it. And the more miserable we all become."

She slumps back down in my arms. I watch her thoughts charge her eyes with energy.

"I wouldn't say that," I argue.

"But you're right—we're taught to love only a few people. We think it's this sacred resource, like we'll run out of it at some point. But the more you love, the more it's returned to you. Hands down. You can't argue with that."

"Maybe," I say. "Or maybe you stop giving it so freely because one day it's taken away and it hurts so much, you need to protect yourself."

She knows what I'm referring to. "Until you realize love's the only thing worth living for in the first place," she says.

She leans back in to me and I wrap my arms around her. Of course I love Dylan. I'm crazy in love with her. But I don't know where she came from and why I deserve her and where this is going to go. I still feel like she's going to wake up one day and look at me. Really look at me. See that I'm not brave, I'm not the male lead in a romantic comedy, see that *she can do better.* Because I think she can. And where would that leave me? Crushed.

\* \* \* \* \*

*I decide to test out her theory that the more you love,* the more it comes back to you. I tell her I love her at Nella's Irish Bar during a heated two-player game of Ms. Pac-Man. I figure if she can pick a strange place and time to tell me, I'm entitled the same liberty. I steal her line. I tell her I love her and Ms. Pac-Man and her better. I finally release the words trapped on the tip of my tongue. It isn't forced and it isn't awkward or embarrassing or even life changing. It just feels right.

Dylan doesn't take her eyes from the screen when I say it. She is about to clear the board and won't be distracted. She just smiles and tells me she loves Ms. Pac-Man too.

# ||| First Question |||

## Gray

*A few days later I check my cell phone* and there's a message from Coach Clark. Coach Clark, as in the head baseball coach at the University of New Mexico, who started recruiting me to play almost two years ago. He leaves this friendly message saying he'd like to talk to me and he wants me to call him back. He leaves his home phone number. He makes it sound like we not only have a past with each other, we have a future.

I call him on my way to work and he sounds genuinely happy to talk to me. Happy. To talk to me. The kid that flaked out of his full-ride scholarship. The kid that let down his coach and his team because he wanted to stay home and be with his family. The schmuck.

We start with small talk. He asks me what I've been up to. Not much. It takes about a minute to fill him in on a year of my life, because not much happens when you're living in a shadow. I didn't start living again until this summer. When someone forced life back into my veins.

He asks me how I'm doing. He dances around the subject behind the question. And for the first time I can truly say things are better. I'm doing better. He's happy to hear that.

He tells me about last season. They ended up fifteen for eight in the conference. The guys are pretty young, but there's a lot of potential and a close team dynamic. They're great guys, he says.

I wonder why he's telling me all this. Is he trying to make me feel guilty? Did he roll out of bed this morning and feel a sudden urge to ruin my day? How thoughtful.

And then he hits me with it.

"Gray, when's the last time you played ball?" he asks.

I don't lie. What's the use?

"I haven't touched a baseball since last fall," I say.

There's a long pause. Awkward silence?

"Do you think you might be ready to pick one up again? We need a pitcher."

I'm too shocked to answer him. I can feel my pulse start to race.

"Gray," he says, "if you want to play, the offer still stands. We'd love to have you on the team." He tells me one of their starting pitchers injured his shoulder last week and needs surgery. He's out for the season, maybe permanently. There's an open spot and he wants me to fill it.

I remind him I'm out of my game. He tells me I can make a comeback, that one season won't set me back too far. He can put me on weight training this fall, some conditioning in the winter. He tells me I'll be ready for the spring if I'm dedicated to working hard every day.

I can still register for classes, he says, and a couple guys on the team share a house and have an extra room this fall if I'm looking for roommates. I'm stunned. It's too easy. Too perfect. Since when does my life work like this?

My fingers turn to noodles. I almost drop the phone.

"Uh," I say. Am I dreaming this conversation? "Coach, what brought all this on?" I ask. "Why are you giving me another chance?"

He clears his throat and tells me it's strange. He got this letter the other day, on the same day he found out he'd lost his pitcher.

"Letter?" I ask.

He said it wasn't signed by anyone, but it mentioned I might be ready to play if the team still wanted me. It said he should give me a call if he's still interested.

"I assume your mom or dad sent it," he says.

I know exactly who wrote it, and I shake my head. "Yeah, you're probably right," I say.

"Listen, Gray," he says. "I want you to know that I'm not upset you gave up the scholarship last year. The whole team understands. But I've had my eye on you for two years. You're the player I want on my roster."

I don't know what to say. My throat feels tight. His voice drops a little.

"When I was your age, my mom passed away. So, I can relate to what happened to you. You made the right decision to stay with your family. I stayed with mine for a while too; I put my life on hold to be with them. But at some point you need to get back in the game, you know?"

I hear him sigh, this heavy sigh like he brought up something he wanted to avoid.

"Yeah," I say.

He says he doesn't need an answer right now. He tells me to think about it. Talk to my parents. Let him know next week. If I want this, and if I'm willing to work for it, I'm on the team. I turn my phone off and stare out the window at a world that's suddenly changed. In five minutes, my life just shifted off-course like it was struck with a meteor, and everything around me is showered in light. Life can change that fast.

* * * * *

*Friday night Dylan and I drive to a coffee shop* in downtown Phoenix called McKinley's to watch an open mike night. Dylan heard it's mostly acoustic. She loves live music and Phoenix has a decent scene. I've taken her to Bash on Ash, Boston's, and the Green Amigo, three bars that let in minors as long as you wear those paper bracelets so the whole world knows you're a baby.

We sit across from each other at a corner table and watch a girl perform "Show Me," by the Cure. She isn't too bad.

Dylan informs me tonight she wants to ask questions. That's it. Questions.

"Like what?" I ask her.

All categories, she says. Just random questions that make you think. She offers to go first. She asks me which albums I would bring if I were stranded on an island and could only bring five CDs.

Next it's my turn. "Okay," I say. "Let's say this island also has an eighty-four-inch TV and DVD player." Dylan rolls her eyes. "Hey," I say. "This is my question. If you could only bring five movies to watch, what would they be?"

And the questions keep rolling and musicians walk on and off the stage and do mike checks and thank us for being there, but we don't really notice. Lately, it's like we're in our own world and it's the safest place I've ever known.

"If you could go out to dinner with any famous person — any living famous person, who would it be?"

"If you wrote a song about your life, what would you title it?"

"If you could date any celebrity, who would it be?"

"If you could shop at any store for free, which one would you choose?"

Dylan proposes another challenge. She pulls her small journal out of her bag. She flips to a blank page and looks at me.

"If you met someone and had to make out their character and you could ask them only ten questions, what would you ask them?" We take turns writing our questions down. We pass the journal back and forth. We cross some out; we star others. We compile our Top Ten list:

1. At the end of the day, what do you want to come home to?

2. Where do you see the world in twenty years?

3. If you could bring one character in a book to life, who would it be?

4. If you could unlearn one thing, what would it be?

5. What's your personal philosophy of life?

6. What do you look for in a friend?

7. If you could travel anywhere, right now, where would you go and what would you do there?

8. If you could design your ideal life, what would it look like?

9. What does family mean to you?

10. If you could be remembered for one thing, what
    would it be?

Dylan and I each add a personal favorite to the list. Dylan's is
*Dogs or cats?* (She claims this answer conveys a critical look into
a person's psyche.) Mine is *Are you a strict vegetarian?* (I can't
hang out with someone who gets offended if I eat steak and bacon
on a regular basis.)

The music ends and Dylan and I head to the Tracks. We sit
under the bridge and Dylan blows bubbles with her Big League
Chew. She lays her head in my lap.

"If you could have one superpower, what would it be?" she
asks.

"That's a great question," I say. "I'd teleport."

I ask her what she would do.

She stares at me, sadly. "I'd control time. I'd make it slow down
or stop completely with the flip of a switch. Like right now," she
says.

We have only three weeks before she's leaving. She's heading
back to Wisconsin to be in her cousin's wedding. Then, she's off on
her next road trip to who knows where.

"My turn," I say. "How long have you been pen pals with
Coach Clark?"

Dylan sits up and her eyes are guilty. "Are you mad?" she
asks.

I stare back at her. Because of her, I get a second shot at my
dream.

"Why would I be mad?"

"I don't know," she says. "For meddling?"

"I got my scholarship back to play baseball. So, yeah, I'm really pissed off at you, Dylan."

I explain everything Coach offered me and that on top of playing I still have time to register for classes, and I can live with some guys on the team.

Dylan's beaming. She doesn't have to ask me what my decision is. It's written on my face.

"Now I just have to break the news to my parents," I say. "There's the challenge."

We're quiet for a moment and Dylan takes out our Top Ten list and starts asking me the questions. My answers are easy. They all revolve around her. What do I want to come home to? Her, naked. What is my ideal way to spend a day? Having sex with her. *All* day. What do I love? Her and Ms. Pac-Man and her better. But I don't want to freak her out, so I try to list other things I love and desire and want to come home to, but all those answers sound forced and trivial and fake. It scares me.

By the time we make it through the list, the sun is climbing into the sky.

# ⅠⅠⅠ FIRST DISCOVER ⅠⅠⅠ

## Dylan

*I wake him up by tracing my finger along his profile.* I've been sleeping over almost every night. It helps that he has a basement entrance and parents who never check on him past dinnertime. I told my aunt the truth—that I fell in love with a desert boy with blue eyes and it's no longer enough to spend every waking moment with him. I need to spend every sleeping moment too.

He opens his eyes and doesn't have to look at me to know I'm restless. "What's the plan?" he asks.

"A little road trip," I say. He sits up and the cotton sheet falls off his bare chest. He stretches his arms out and rubs his eyes and pulls his fingers through his messy tangle of hair. He asks me where we're going.

"Sedona."

**✳ ✳ ✳ ✳ ✳**

*Sedona's a canyon town north of Phoenix,* hidden inside tall walls of pink rock. As you drive north, the brown desert hills of central Arizona slowly transform into a pinkish-red valley. You feel like you've taken a wrong turn, fallen off the earth, and landed somewhere closer to Mars.

We pull over five or six times before we even hit the city limits so I can capture panoramic shots. Gray never rushes me; he never questions why I want to take a photo. He never holds me back. He waits next to the car while I aim my camera at a stack of red rocks, pinned up under a blue sky. I tell Gray I'm going to make his dad a coffee table book of my summer photography.

"You've never even met my dad," he says. "Why do you want to give him a present?"

I climb onto the roof of the car to get a better angle, and he watches me crouch down to take a picture. I wait until a minivan moves out of the frame.

"You said he likes travel photography," I point out.

"Do you ever think about yourself?" Gray asks.

"Sure."

He tells me he finds that hard to believe. I look out at the curving highway that snakes through the red valley and disappears inside a shadowed crevice of rocks. I love the way the road twists and fades in the distance, like it's alive. It makes me want to chase it.

"I think about the people I'm going to meet. Where I'm going to end up," I say, and zoom in on a pink and white striped rock wall that looks like a candy cane.

"Wouldn't it be nice to know?" he asks.

I take the picture and hop off the car. "I love not knowing. My entire life has been predictable," I say. "I just want to imagine it for a while."

Gray studies me for a few seconds and slowly nods before he turns and gets back in the car.

When we pull into downtown, we stop at a café called Brew with a View, a shop with stucco brown exterior and tall glass windows that look out at a red mountain called Bell Rock. I lean over the counter and ask the barista if he's local, and when he says he is, I ask him where he recommends spending the day in Sedona. On the drive up, I told Gray that I detest travel books. How is surrounding yourself with a crowd of other tourists an authentic experience? It isn't traveling. It's just standing in line. You need to hit up the locals for the best spots.

The barista grins at us, his bright white teeth framed by tan, leathery skin. "What do you want to see?" he asks.

What I always want to see. "A place I'll never forget," I say. The barista looks at Gray.

"She's optimistic," he notes.

"You have no idea," Gray says.

"I want to know the secret spots," I say. "Not the tourist traps."

He hesitates for a second, but then he grabs a brown paper bag off the counter and draws a map to a vortex called Heather's Knoll. He tells us tourists rarely go there; it's more of a local meditation spot. I ask him if we can get there on bikes. He nods and I thank him and reach for Gray's hand. When we walk outside, I examine the map.

"What's a vortex?" I wonder out loud. I hadn't expected an answer, but Gray explains it's a power spot and supposedly Sedona is full of them.

"What do you mean, 'power spot'?" I ask, and he tells me there's magnetic energy moving through the earth and supposedly these energy fields connect at certain places around the world, and Sedona is one of them. People think it has healing powers.

We head toward a bike rental shop and pass crystal sellers and bookstores, healing centers and acupuncturists.

I ask him if he believes in that sort of thing, and he shrugs.

"I'm not really into New Age stuff," he says. But he tells me people from all over the world travel to Sedona to meditate or pray. He explains vortexes are considered more spiritual than anything. It's a place where you can feel more in tune with the universe, that if you sit still and listen long enough, you'll hear answers to your questions.

We walk into the Golden Word bookstore and I buy a book on Sedona vortexes written by a local author. I pick out a postcard for Gray of a car crushed under the weight of a huge cactus. I buy my mom a sterling silver ring and my sister a bookmark picturing Cathedral Rock, the famous red cliffs in Sedona that look like church steeples. Gray gets me a postcard featuring Snoopy Rock because he likes the name of it.

We stop to order sandwiches at the Black Cow Café and we fill our water bottles for the ride. Sedona is a city of hills, and in the ten-mile bike ride, we steadily climb. We stop twice for water breaks and once so I can photograph a snake slithering across the road. As we travel farther away from downtown, I'm more aware of the silence. I can't hear anything except the sound of our pedals inching us forward and the rubber tires gripping the asphalt. It's as if we're inside a dream dipped in red ink. The barista told us about this—he said we'd be surprised by the silence around a vortex.

We find the dirt road he drew out, marked only by a green sign bleached from the sun. We can barely make out the word HEATHER. We turn and pedal up a red gravel road, until we reach a dirt parking lot where the ground is padded smooth. We hop off our bikes and lean them against a tree trunk. We don't worry about locking them up. We don't worry about anything.

A sign in the parking lot reads RESPECT THE SILENCE. I grab Gray's hand and we follow a dirt trail that winds through a tunnel of trees. We pass a circle constructed on the ground, outlined with smooth round rocks. The circle is divided up into pieces, like a pie. I whisper and ask Gray what it is. He tells me it's a medicine wheel, used for meditation.

"It's supposed to create positive energy," he says. "I think Native Americans started it." He tells me each piece of the wheel represents different people coming together. It's about respecting people and creating a peaceful balance in the universe. I watch him with surprise.

"You said you weren't into New Age stuff. How do you know all this?"

He smiles. "Amanda loved Sedona," he says. "We used to drive up here every summer. That book you bought downtown, she owned the same one." I feel my shoulders sink.

"Why didn't you tell me? We didn't have to come here," I say, and he tells me it's okay. He wants to be here.

"I've never seen this spot before," he says. He pulls me along and we pass another sign saying, QUIET: FOR PRAYER AND MEDITATION. The path opens up to several lookouts, but I keep going. Gray follows me and I veer off the trail, where the trees open up and warm, flat rocks rise out over a high cliff. We walk out to the edge and I inhale a deep breath and soak in the silence. The air feels different out here — lighter, crisper, charged with energy.

We're surrounded by a rusty canyon that's streaked with black and gray rocks. It looks ancient, as if we're standing at the feet of a philosopher. I stare out at the beauty that embraces us and feel one thing. Humbled. It puts me in my place to know these rocks have existed thousands of years before me and they'll survive thousands of years after I'm gone. It makes me feel inconsequential. My problems become so small and meaningless they evaporate and blow away in the desert air.

So many people worry their lives away. They take themselves so seriously. They try to fight time and aging and gravity and death. They spend so much time stressing and planning and over-planning that they miss out on living. I never want to be like that. I never want to waste time. After all, we're just passing observers, as insignificant to these giant formations as a speck of dust. So we might as well appreciate the view and enjoy the journey.

I feel weightless. I wonder if this is what people mean about the magic of Sedona, if this realization is the vortex whispering a secret to me.

A thin layer of sweeping clouds touches the tip of the canyon peaks, and green trees grow deep in the shaded rocks underneath us. I can hear only my breaths. We sit down on the warm rocks and take off our shoes and eat our sandwiches, whispering a little back and forth but mostly just absorbing the air around us and honoring the silence.

We lie out on the rocks for the rest of the afternoon and let the sun lull us into contentment, and even Gray quietly admits there's a healing energy to this place.

# Gray

*We eat dinner in Sedona at the Red Planet Café,* an alien-themed restaurant. We're greeted as earthlings by our waitress as she hands us plastic menus that look like they glow in the dark. I order the Mars attack sandwich, the cyclone fries, and a moon milk shake. Dylan orders the Neptune wrap. We drink out of glowing green straws, and fluorescent alien heads stare down at us from the ceiling. Our table looks like a satellite orbiting space, and our seats look like huge eggshells cut perfectly in half. Electronic music plays around us, as if we're trapped inside a Super Mario game.

Dylan thinks the atmosphere is funky. I think it's creepy. We agree to combine our descriptions and call it crunky.

We're both flushed from a full day in the sun, and strokes of pink color Dylan's nose and cheekbones. I wonder how warm her lips are. I'm eager to find out. I bet she has some great tan lines after today. I'm anxious to see those, too. I plan on tracing every inch of them with my finger.

When we leave Sedona the sky is turning a bluish black. The red rocks, gray in the distance, look like dinosaurs curled up to sleep. While we drive, Dylan asks me what I was thinking about at Heather's Knoll. We spent hours there, and I was shocked Dylan managed to stay quiet for so long. She didn't exactly sit still. She spent most of the time writing in her journal and investigating the other paths around the vortex with her camera. But she rarely spoke.

I look out the window and stall. I don't want to admit to what I was really thinking all day. When Dylan was leaning back on the warm rock, her eyes closed against the sun, my mind was fixated on her. And I was pretty much thinking about one thing: sex. Wondering if she wants to have it. When. With me? We sleep together every night. I've seen her naked. But she always pulls back. She lets me in on everything else. Her secrets. Her soul. But now I want it all. And it's driving me crazy.

I think about having sex with her every other second. I consider it a healthy obsession. I have a box of condoms shoved away in a desk drawer that I bought two years ago. "Ribbed for a woman's pleasure." Unopened. Taunting me.

I decide to tell Dylan I wasn't thinking about anything. I was trying to empty my mind.

"What about you?" I ask. She also stalls before she answers, and then admits she was thinking about my family. I can feel the mood shift in the car. There's a serious edge to Dylan's voice.

My guard instinctively takes over. Once you invest in people, once you let them in, they feel entitled to make your problems their own. And I don't want that. I don't need that. Not right now.

# ǀǀǀ First Fight ǀǀǀ

## Dylan

*I blurt out the question before I lose my nerve.*

"Have you gone through any counseling since Amanda died?"
I ask. A few weighted seconds crawl by.

"Counseling?" Gray repeats, his voice hard. He's already on
the defensive. "Where is *this* coming from? I haven't gone through
counseling," he insists, as if this would be weak. As if it would label him as something.

"Has your mom or dad?" I ask, and I try to keep my tone light,
as if this is a casual conversation. He sees it as more of an inter-
rogation.

"No," he says flatly. "I don't know. I doubt it." He's glaring at
my profile, and I try to concentrate on the road, but I can still feel
the heat from his eyes. "We don't need to see a therapist," he adds.
"Not that my family's psychological condition is any of your business."

Period. End of the counseling discussion. But I won't give up.
I keep my voice calm and try to water down his anger. I tell him
that talking to someone could help his family work through this,
learn how to cope and make it easier for his parents to transition
after he leaves town.

He takes such a sharp breath, I swear his chest is on fire. "Did you get that off a grieving pamphlet?"

"No," I say quietly.

"What do you know about coping, Dylan?" he shoots back. "Who are *you* to tell me *I* need therapy?" he says, as if I'm the crazy one. "Are you saying I'm depressed?"

"No, I didn't say that, and even if you were, it's nothing to be ashamed of. You've been through a tragedy. All I'm saying is, it's okay to ask people for help."

"Well, I don't need to pay a shrink just to hear someone tell me life's going to be okay."

I take a long, deep breath and tell him that's the problem. Life isn't okay, and denying it won't help.

"Sometimes you need professionals to help you work through things," I say.

Gray raises his hands. "I can't believe I'm hearing this," he says. He crosses his arms tightly over his chest to contain them.

"There are counselors who have worked with hundreds of people in your shoes," I say. "They can give your family advice on how to deal with all this."

He glares at me like my words are a slap across his face. "I don't need any advice. I'm fine."

"I'm worried about your parents," I say.

"Why?" he asks.

"Doesn't it feel good to finally talk about Amanda?"

He nods once.

"Don't you think it would help your parents if they could talk about her?" I try to keep my voice smooth. I crossed a line by making his family's personal business my own. But isn't that what friendship is? Isn't that what love is? It's more than caring and laughing and inspiring. It's about taking hurt and anger off people's shoulders and helping to carry the weight. It's more important to love people on their worst days than their best.

"Don't concern yourself with my parents, Dylan. You don't even know them. Stop buying them gifts and trying to surprise them. It's weird. You can't care about people you don't know. Maybe *you're* the one who should see a therapist."

I know he doesn't mean it. He's trying to steer the conversation away from himself, even if it means attacking me. "I care about you," I say. "And I know you're worried about your parents. Isn't that why you're still in Phoenix?"

He presses his lips together, and then opens them to almost shout, "They don't need counseling. This is none of your business, so drop it." It's more than a subtle hint. But I'm already submerged waist deep. I might as well dive in.

"I just think your mom and dad could use an outlet," I say. "Maybe you guys could meet with a therapist as a family?"

"What's a shrink going to do? Tell us to keep a journal and find a happy place?"

"No."

"Diagnose us with some grieving disorder and prescribe a bottle of artificial mood enhancer? Fuck *that*."

I have to fight to keep my voice calm, and I meet his glaring eyes: "Going to a counselor isn't a weak thing to do. That's your problem. You see it as desperate."

"Whatever."

"Have you ever thought that going to a counselor with your parents is maybe the bravest thing you could do?" I ask. "The most loving thing? The most selfless thing? If you feel so responsible about helping them deal with Amanda's death, then maybe this is something you need to do for them. This isn't just about you."

He starts to yell.

"What do you know about what we're going through? Nothing! I'm not going to spill my feelings to some counselor who's just going to sit there and see me as another sad kid who lost his sister. Just another tragic family dealing with death. Because this isn't just any sister. Or any daughter."

He slams his fist on the dashboard.

"It's my sister," he shouts. "It's Amanda. And my life is never going to be the same again. Don't tell me to listen to some stranger say that I need to get over it and I need to move on. Because if they ever knew Amanda, if you knew her, you'd get it."

"What would I get?" I ask.

"That she deserves to have us miss her every single day. Even if it tortures us. She deserves that."

My throat is tight. I take a shaky breath.

"I'm only going to say this once, because I love you and I think you need to hear it."

I look over at him and see that his jaw is set tight. He's facing forward and his eyes are closed.

"You need to live your life, Gray. You need to live for the future again. Amanda isn't coming back. I'm not saying you have to forget about her. But you have to move on," I say. "You're not the one who died."

He tells me to shut up before he smashes the window.

"Fine," I say, and my voice sounds torn. I bite my lips together to stop them from shaking. I focus on the white lines of the road ahead.

Gray turns up the stereo. He pulls his sweatshirt hood low over his head so he can block out the things he doesn't want to see and the questions he doesn't want to face. He's trying to disappear again.

# ╎╎╎ First Forgive ╎╎╎

## Gray

*I'm fine.*

But I can't turn my brain off. Six hours later.

I'm fine.

Why did she have to go there? We had the most incredible day. The most incredible summer. Why did she have to strike the one nerve that would make me lash out like that? I know I hurt her. I could hear it in her voice. And all she did was call me out on the things I need to hear. All she did was care. I'm such an asshole.

I'm fine.

I roll over in bed and stare out my window. I watch the moon in the sky; it looks so peaceful and far away, and that's where I want to be. It's been six hours. I miss her. She's usually in my arms at this time. My bed feels too big for my single body. It's swallowing me.

I sit up and kick off my covers. I throw a pair of shorts on over my boxers and slip on some flip-flops. I walk out into the hot night. It has to be close to a hundred degrees, even at three in the morning. The dry grass cracks under my sandals like straw.

I drive to her house through dark, lifeless streets. I blast the Killers from my rolled-down window and try to focus on the music instead of the guilt clogging my mind. I feel like smoking again, like filling my lungs with something toxic, because my whole body feels toxic. I hate that I can't take back what I said. I would never hit Dylan. I would never hurt her. But I just beat her up with words. And I'm supposed to sleep after that? Sleep doesn't come to people who have a heavy apology resting on their heart. Sleep knows better.

I pull up to the curb next to her house and stare at the dark windows. I turn off the engine, walk around to the back, and grab some gravel rocks from the landscape bordering the patio. I throw a small piece up and it ricochets off her window with a loud tap. I've done this before. It's our prehistoric-style telephone call.

I throw another rock, and a few seconds later a dim light fills the window of her room. Dylan pulls the curtains back and I look up to see her silhouette in the frame.

She doesn't have to ask who it is. She doesn't even have to acknowledge me. She could be mad, she could be stubborn. She could hold a grudge, could hold me at arm's length. I close my eyes and pray she doesn't. Life's too short to hold back forgiveness. And we only have a few more weeks together. I map out my apology once more while I wait for her to come down.

She makes it easy for me. We sit on the wicker couch outside and she rests her head in my lap and listens while I tell her she was right, that she said exactly what I needed to hear and she's the one person in my life who has the balls to confront me. And I'm not saying it just to win her back. I mean every word of it. I tell her I spent an hour online looking at counselors in Phoenix. I tell her I need to talk to my parents about it; I just needed someone to kick me hard enough to do it. And I thank her for loving me enough to say the hard things.

She's half asleep in my lap, her face as serene as an angel's in the moonlight. I trace my fingers along her smooth skin, and it feels like warm porcelain. I tell her I'm sorry I flipped out. I said things I didn't mean. Dylan slowly lifts herself up, and her sleepy eyes meet mine.

"I love you, Gray," she says. "And I love that you care about your parents. But you're stuck here and you hate it. You're not doing anybody any good."

"Yeah," I say, and I rest my head against the back of the chair and look up at the sky. It's easy to hear words. It's another thing to accept them.

"You can't live for your parents. You're not responsible for making them happy. They need to do that on their own. You need to work on you. That's enough for you to handle right now."

I nod.

"If your sister were sitting here right now, what would she tell your family to do?"

I sigh, and my nose prickles as tears tease the back of my eyes. I tell Dylan she'd want me to get the hell out of here. She'd tell my mom to stop using work as an escape. She'd tell my dad to stop scheduling so many business trips as an excuse to avoid the house.

"You know what I admire about you?" Dylan says. "You're a survivor. And you're a lot stronger than you give yourself credit for. You just don't see it."

I shake my head and tell her she only sees the best in people. I'm not that strong.

"My dad walked out on my mom when I was little," Dylan says.

"What?" I say. I stare at Dylan. How, in all this time, has she never mentioned this? She tells me she can barely remember him. He left when she was four years old and he met her a few years ago and said he was sorry and he was sober now and he wanted to reconnect, to be there for her and her sister. But then he never called again. And it's okay, she says. Her mom remarried this wonderful man who's always been a father to her.

Dylan tells me she's only bringing it up because she's so amazed at how her mom dealt with being abandoned. Her mom showed her that when life hands you tragedy, you can do two things with it. You can let it kick you down and make you weak and turn you into a victim. Or you can have hope that you'll get through it and there's still something amazing to live for.

"That's what my mom did," Dylan says. "She survived. She was angry and regretted marrying him, but she didn't dwell on it. She let it go and focused on the future. She could have been bitter and turned me off to love and family because it can be just misery and heartache. But she didn't."

Dylan tells me victims don't make it very far in life.

"But I know that's not you," she says.

"How do you know that?" I ask.

She shrugs. "Because you let me in."

I nod and wrap my fingers around hers. Dylan rests her head on my shoulder and we watch the sunlight creep over the horizon and run out above us in the sky. I'm finally beginning to understand why this misguided angel has stumbled into my life, and for the first time, I'm starting to believe I deserve her.

# ||| FIRST CONFRONT |||

## Gray

*My mom and dad* are in the family room *at the same time.* I haven't seen them together in months. It's now or never. I walk in the room and stand between them. My dad's sitting in a recliner, hiding behind the newspaper, and my mom's grading papers on the love seat. The news is on. Someone was kidnapped in Tempe. A girl from ASU is missing. Five more local businesses closed. Fun, uplifting stories.

Dylan and I played out the scenario several times. She played my parents and acted out different reactions. She was hurt, she was angry, she was suspicious, she was hysterical. She made me rehearse for hours.

I sit down on the couch opposite my mom, across from my dad, and we form an asymmetrical triangle. I wait for them to notice to me. And they don't. I observe my dad's face over the newspaper. He's gained weight since Amanda died. More business trips. More fast food. And he's aged. His hair is thinner, lighter, with streaks of gray. My mom's lost weight. Her face is tight and gaunt. Her skin is pale. I realize we've all been slowly dying.

Then I think, Why *am* I here? Why am I neglecting my life

when they don't even notice me? Dylan was right. This isn't doing any of us any good. A pulse of courage jumps through my veins and pushes against my heart.

I clear my throat, and when I have their attention the words pour out. I tell them everything. I tell them I want all of us to meet with a counselor. I'm tired of living in the shadow of Amanda's death and letting her memory pull a curtain between us and the rest of the world. I tell them we aren't doing Amanda any honor by giving up, by dying ourselves. We are the ones that are living. So it's about time we got around to doing it.

They both stare at me as if I'm a stranger in their son's body. I've never stood up to them before. Confrontation isn't common in my family. Respect is obedience. Don't question authority. Accept it. But back then I always had Amanda. I had her to vent to when I needed to disagree. She *was* my family. She pumped life into us, around us. It was her love that made us all connect. We're withering away without her, like plants without roots.

My dad sets down his paper. He crosses his arms and asks me what this is all about.

"I want to play baseball again," I say. I repeat my entire conversation with Coach Clark and I list all the reasons I should accept the offer. I tell him I'd regret passing it up this time.

My dad's silent. My mom's skeptical. A minute crawls by before anyone speaks up.

"You've been out of baseball a long time, Gray," Mom says.

I tell her it's more than baseball. I want my life back. I want to go to school and start over. I want to have a future.

"It's that girl you met, isn't it?" my dad asks. "You want to follow that girl."

I throw my hands up in the air and tell them I have a full-ride scholarship. What part of this don't they get? I neglect to mention that I plan on asking Dylan to move out to New Mexico with me. And I'm pretty confident she'll do it.

My mom tells me it isn't as easy as it sounds. That escaping to Albuquerque won't instantly fix all my problems. I tighten my lips and thank God Dylan brought up this same point a few days ago. She predicted my mom might cave in, that she'd reach for the excuse that I'm running away because she'd rather have me here, miserable, than lose me. It's true what they say, that misery loves company. When Dylan tested this response, I reacted by punching the wall of my bedroom. Now I can handle it with a little more maturity.

I tell them I know it won't be easy, and I'm not trying to escape. I take a deep breath and stand up.

"I'm not asking for your permission," I say. "I am doing this." They both stare at me and my dad's frowning and my mom's eyes are filling with tears.

"But your support would mean everything to me," I add. "And I know Amanda would want me to do this."

They're both silent. I ask for one more thing.

"I want all of us to meet with a counselor before I leave," I say. I slap a piece of paper down on the table. It lists three counselors Dylan and I narrowed down from our research. I stand my ground and wait. I remind myself that this is heading in the right direction. I need to be the brave one.

My mom just stares at the piece of paper as if it's a hornet she wants to crush. I would have done the same thing a few days ago. My dad's face is deadpan and his eyes are frozen, staring down at the ground. At least no one's screaming. I leave the room because I understand what they need. It's what I needed after Dylan confronted me about all this. Time.

* * * * *

*We're sitting out on the concrete foundation* we discovered on Camelback Mountain. We've come out here a few times. We need to make the most of the view from our dining room before it becomes a workout gym for one of the Diamondback baseball players or Arizona Cardinals (our prediction of who owns this spot). Tonight we brought a blanket and spread it out underneath us. I'm trying not to think about the dwindling days we have left together. I'd rather focus my energy on more productive thoughts—like how to keep Dylan from leaving.

I ask her where she sees herself in five years.

"I have no idea," she says, and confesses she has trouble planning a week ahead, let alone five years.

I tap my foot on the ground. "But don't you want to plant roots eventually?" I'm hopeful. I want her roots to have the same city limits as mine. At least the same area code. Preferably a New Mexico area code.

"Not any time soon," she says.

I try a different angle. "What about a job? You have to make money."

Dylan leans back on her elbows and thinks about this.

"Money's okay, but it's not the most important thing on my list. Cars are great, and nice clothes, and five-star restaurants. But I've always been more impressed with the sky. With canyons and trees and mountains. I'd rather invest my time collecting memories and friends and love and all the things money can't buy."

I can't help but smile. So much for having a practical conversation with this girl. I'm consciously savoring the time I have left with her because I know it's drawing to a close. She has no idea how intriguing she is to me. How smart and fascinating and unpredictable and magnetic. And she's singled me out as her lucky audience.

I ask Dylan what she thinks about when she's alone.

"You want to know what I mostly think about?" she asks, and her eyes meet mine.

"I think about you," she says. She leans closer to me and holds one of my hands inside her smaller ones and examines it like it's a map to some mysterious world. She tells me she thinks about my lips and my eyes and my skinny long legs.

I inform her that she's the one with skinny long legs. Mine are toned.

She smiles and says she loves my big hands and long fingers with veins wrapping around the knuckles like a vine. She slowly traces each vein with her index finger and it makes my heart race. She tells me she loves my long eyelashes and my toes and the patch of hair on my chest.

"Is there anything you don't like about me?" I ask, because I want to know how to be better. How to be half the person she is. Then she looks at me like I'm crazy and tells me she loves everything about me. I wonder how that can be possible, but then I think maybe when it's right, this is exactly how it should feel.

"What random thing did you do today?" I ask. It's my favorite question.

"Today it was more of a random thought."

I wait for her to continue.

"I thought about the best way to be born," she says simply, as if this is a normal thing to contemplate. "If you could choose how you come into the world, how would you want to be born? It's your most important entrance; you want to make it count. Imagine if you could be hatched from an egg—wouldn't that be cool? To crack out, to stretch your arms and legs and break through walls? That would be a memorable entrance, not the crying, screaming, terrified way humans are squeezed out into the world."

"I guess it's not ideal," I say.

"If I could be born any way, I'd be a raindrop," she says. "I'd begin in a cloud and start with a peaceful descent and then gain speed on the way down to earth. Then I'd land in a forest and I'd grow like a cabbage patch kid."

I don't interrupt, because she's in some crazy trance now.

"Then a stork would pick me up when I'm just this tiny baby and he'd wrap me in flannel sheets and fly me home. He'd tell me stories on the way, about oceans and carnivals and love and family and I'd fall asleep to the rhythmic flapping of his giant wings. When I woke up, my parents would be holding me. Amazed at this miracle breathing in their arms."

Then, as if this isn't enough, she says her other random thought for the day is what animal she'd like to be.

"But the more I think about it, the more I'm convinced I love being human," she says.

This surprises me. I figured she'd want to be a bird. Something with wings. "Why?"

"We have it the best," she says. "Think about it. First, we're bipedal. And I like being tall. Imagine being quadrupedal. You wouldn't be able to walk hand in hand. Or have your hands free to take pictures. How boring would that be?"

I admit I've never thought about it.

"And being a mammal is crucial. I'd hate to live in the water. No hiking in the sun. No road trips. No running and Rollerblading and feeling the wind in your hair. And I can't swim very well," she adds.

"And imagine being nocturnal. No more sitting back and enjoying sunsets or feeling the sun on your skin or studying the clouds in the sky. And humans have the largest brains. Think if we had a tiny cat brain? No analyzing, philosophizing, writing, reading, dreaming. I can't imagine that."

"We wouldn't be having this conversation," I point out. "What a loss that would be." She catches me roll my eyes and she lifts her hand up to slap me but I grab it in mine and squeeze and press my lips to hers before she can argue.

# ⅠⅠⅠ FIRST INSPIRE ⅠⅠⅠ

## Dylan

*Friday night I'm over at Gray's and we're watching TV.* But I have a problem watching television — I prefer to make it interactive. So, during the commercials we turn the volume down and do our own voice-overs for the actors. We turn a shampoo commercial into an ad for killing head lice. We transform a Kentucky Fried Chicken commercial into a public service announcement about diabetes.

I wander into Gray's room and he follows as if we're attached by an invisible cord. Lately, it feels like we are. I turn on his stereo and tell him I want to listen to music.

He plays me his favorite. Acoustic. The guitar, he argues, is the best instrument. He says you can go without any other instrument and write any song imaginable. A guitar can wail, it can cry. It can drum, it can laugh. It has every range of emotions, like it's part human.

He plays Ryan Adams's album *Heartbreaker* and we turn the lights off and lie on the floor next to the speakers. We spend hours listening, just listening. We hear every beat, every clever layering of instruments. The carpeting absorbs the bass and howl of the harmonica and the heartbeat of the drums. Gray's fingers dance against mine and I memorize his hands. I'm relaxed, but I'm too high to fall asleep. The music falls around us like rain and it melts over our skin and into our bones. We imagine what he was thinking when he wrote each song. We dissect the meaning of the lyrics. We listen to what the music is saying.

It's the best date I've ever had.

I get up and turn on Gray's desk lamp and study a corkboard hung on the wall. He uses it to tack up ticket stubs from all the concerts he's been to. I read the concerts out loud.

"Black Crowes, the Killers, the Roots, Atmosphere, U2, Beastie Boys, Bob Dylan, Ryan Adams, Tom Petty, Paul Simon, Red Hot Chili Peppers, the Counting Crows, the Flaming Lips . . .

"Where did you see all these shows?" I ask. He tells me mostly in Phoenix, a few in Vegas. Some in Los Angeles. My eyes perk up at this.

"I've always wanted to see L.A.," I tell him. He says it's only a six-hour drive. I look down at him and he's lying on the floor, his arms folded behind his head. He doesn't have to see my plotting smile—he can sense the question. His summer school classes are over and we both know he has the weekend off from work.

"When do you want to go?" he asks, his eyes on the ceiling.

"Can we leave in the morning?" I ask.

"You're crazy," he says.

I nod in agreement and crawl back down on the carpet to join him. *Tell me something I don't know,* I'm about to say, but his hands tug me on top of him and his warm lips are on mine too fast for the words to slip out.

✳ ✳ ✳ ✳ ✳

*We head out at an ungodly hour (according to Gray),* but I can't sleep when L.A. is waiting to be discovered. We stop for gas and slam coffee to keep us awake for the long drive, then head west, through the Mojave Desert.

We're in L.A. by the afternoon and we drive straight into Santa Monica, where we check in to a hotel on the coast. Between the two of us we have enough money to splurge on a small ocean view room. We stand out on our narrow balcony and stare at the crashing waves like they're part of a foreign world. When you spend your summer in a landlocked city like Phoenix, the ocean has a strange effect. On the hottest summer days it's easy to think the world has dried up, that the relief of rain is a myth. Seeing an endless body of water spread out against the horizon instead of a cracked desert plain is like turning your world upside down.

I change in the bathroom, and when I come out, Gray blinks as if he doesn't recognize me. His mouth slowly falls open as his eyes trace my outfit.

I run my hands over my silky hips. "It's just a dress," I say. But I know what he's thinking—it's short and black and hugs me in all the right places. My mom and sister forced the dress on me last year, claiming that clothes are like bait. This is my first time wearing it, and it proves their theory right. From Gray's expression, I'd guess he wants to do one thing: Rip it off. I even combed my hair straight and put on some mascara and eyeliner and lipgloss. For me, it's a monumental transformation.

"You own a dress?" he says, and I stare at him like it's a stupid question.

"Every girl needs to own a little black dress," I tell him, as if it's a law. I pull him out of the room before he gets the chance to molest me. We'll save that for later.

We cross Ocean Drive and pass restaurants and souvenir shops. We walk past a bike lane busy with skaters and runners, and finally we reach the warm, sandy beach. We watch seagulls ride the wind as if they're floating on an invisible wave in the sky and we wade into the cold, curling water. We walk down Santa Monica Pier and people watch and look at amateur artwork. We ask strangers to take our picture while we do awkward prom poses, with Gray standing behind me and wrapping his arms around my waist as we both force tense smiles.

We hop into Gray's car and drive downtown so he can introduce me to the most famous street in Los Angeles—Sunset Boulevard. We eat sushi at Miyagi's and sit outside to watch the constant stream of traffic crawl down the strip. He points out the Viper Room, the Roxy Theatre, and the Whiskey Bar, and talks about the bands that made them famous.

We walk past Armani and Prada boutiques. We walk into Book Soup and browse the ceiling-high shelves stacked with screenplays. We sit down in the corner and read out loud the opening scene from *Pulp Fiction*. We head outside and see the Sky Bar and the Comedy Store and the House of Blues and point out the Porches, Ferraris, and endless limos that speed by. We pretend to see celebrities.

We drive down to Hollywood Boulevard to see the Mann Chinese Theater. We get Vanilla Ice Blendeds at the Coffee Bean on the corner of Hollywood and Orange. We take pictures on the Walk of Stars and buy CDs from artists promoting their albums on the street. We buy each other fake Oscars at a souvenir shop. Gray picks out "Best Director" for me and I buy him "Best Vocal Performer."

We walk hand in hand outside the Kodak Theater, bustling with tourists and shoppers. We stare at the blinking cinema lights of the old theaters and watch searchlights rotate in the sky above us like planets circling on a wild orbit.

When we're both exhausted, we drive back to Santa Monica, but I insist on seeing the ocean at night, so we head down to the beach. It's the perfect place to end the perfect day.

And to bring up a thought that's been plaguing my mind.

# ⅠⅠⅠ FIRST TIME ⅠⅠⅠ

## Gray

*The waves are white against the black horizon* and rise up only to crash down like angry fists. Dylan and I sit on the sand and watch the free performance. We're both quiet, and I wrap my arm around her shoulders. I lean close to her and rub my lips back and forth along her jaw line and slowly work my way down her neck. I feel her shudder. She tells me I'm missing the ocean and it's beautiful. I tell her she's more beautiful. My other hand's resting on her leg. I slowly slide it up, under her dress, and I can feel her thigh break out in goose bumps.

I hear her breaths shorten and I smile to myself. I've never been very smooth with women. Or confident. But with Dylan I am.

"I want to give you something," she says suddenly. I look into her eyes and they're wild, intense, but with a hint of seriousness. I tell her I'd love anything. I tickle her neck with the tip of my nose. I tell her I'd love a book on tractors now that I've finished the one on mullets. I wait for her to come back with something. When I look at her she isn't smiling, and I realize this is something serious.

"What is it?" I ask.

She tells me it's something you can only give one time, to one person. My heart pounds and my eyebrows shoot up.

"Yeah?" I manage to say.

"Yeah," she says with a smile.

"Are you sure?" I ask her.

"I love you," she says. "I love you more than I've ever loved anyone. And I wouldn't regret it. I would regret not doing it. So I want to give it to you."

I grab her hand and pull her up. I have to make an effort not to sprint back to the hotel. My mind's spinning. I'm going to have sex? I'm going to have sex! Holy shit. Holy shit. I'm going to have sex. Should we buy condoms? Where should we buy condoms? Why didn't I bring the damn condoms?!

We walk with long strides across the sand and the hotel slowly inches toward us, but not fast enough, like it's teasing me. As if she can read my mind, Dylan informs me she packed condoms. I almost pick her up and swing her in circles at hearing the second greatest news of my life. But I'm too fixated on getting back to our room.

"Is that dirty?" she asks.

I grin and a self-assured smile crosses her face. "Yes, it's dirty, and I love you for it."

She tells me she's wanted to have sex for a while. She just wanted it to be a surprise.

*Okay, that's good,* I tell myself. It's not just a spontaneous idea. She's been considering this, so there's no question she wants to do it. We walk into the lobby of the hotel and I try not to grin at the man behind the counter. I refrain from screaming, "I'm going to have sex! With this gorgeous woman. She wants to have sex. I didn't even have to ask, she just wants to have sex. With me! Can you believe it?" I take deep breaths and try to downplay that this moment is the highlight of my life. Air kicks and high-fives probably wouldn't be a cool move right now.

\* \* \* \* \*

*We walk down the hallway* and take the elevator up to the third floor. My hand's sweating in Dylan's, but her fingers are loose and relaxed. Doesn't anything make this girl nervous?

I fumble with the key card and finally open the door. A breeze blows the curtain into the room. I shut the door and put the Do Not Disturb sign on the outside handle. I smile. I've always wanted to do that.

I turn and look at Dylan. She's standing a few feet away, studying me with a small grin. Is this going to be awkward? Should I just throw myself at her? Will she want to take it slow? Should I undress myself or let her do it? Maybe I should stop standing here looking like a clueless idiot before she changes her mind.

She sits on the bed and keeps her eyes steady on mine. She slowly slips her shoes off one at a time. Oh, my God. Since when is Dylan this sexy? So why am I standing here like a human-size brick?

I tell Dylan I have to go to the bathroom. I shut the door and try to pee, but my dick's already sticking straight up at the ceiling. Great. I'm sure she caught *that* minor detail. We haven't even kissed yet. I shake my head and do my best to pee. I pull my pants back up, trying to make my hard-on less obvious. I stare at myself in the mirror and splash cold water on my face to calm down. My face is flushed.

I concentrate on one critical thing. Last, Gray. You've got to make it last. No two pumps, you're done. Don't be that guy. You're stronger than that.

Think sports.

Try to name every candy bar you can.

Think about anything but what her body feels like, because as soon as you let yourself go there, it's over.

Enough with the pep talk. I take a deep breath. This is it. It's what you were born to do.

I open the bathroom door and Dylan's sitting there, her legs crossed, leaning back on her hands, her long arms supporting her weight. She could be the poster girl for composed confidence, and I'm a little jealous. She has the condoms sitting on the bed next to her. I look down at them and bite my lips. Will she want to put it on for me? Oh, that could be weird. What if she doesn't know how and I have to walk her through it like a health class teacher? I stare back at Dylan and hesitate. Why am I so nervous? Come on, Gray. Use your animal instincts here.

"Are you sure?" I ask again.

I don't want her to feel pressured. I've heard girls change their mind at the last minute. Panic. I can understand. They're the ones letting us inside. They feel the pain more than the pleasure, at least the first time. I don't want Dylan to feel any pain. That thought almost makes me lose all my nerve.

She stands up from the bed and steps toward me. She reaches her arms around my neck. She reassures me with a kiss that starts out slow but then she opens her lips and I stop thinking and suddenly all I'm capable of sensing is how she feels and how she tastes. My fingers curl around her hips and I pull at her dress and squeeze the fabric until it balls up in my fists and I really want to rip it off. We fall back on the bed.

I don't have to worry about anything because it's Dylan, it's me—it's perfect. We can't be wrong together. This realization gives me the confidence to take the lead. To pull her clothes off. To show Dylan how much I love her.

# ||| FIRST BREATHE |||

## Dylan

*We stretch out on the bed, naked,* with the blankets kicked off and only each other's body heat warming the mattress. My breaths are still short. So are his. It's the only sound I can hear. My heart's kicking against my chest. The room is dark, lit only by the street lights outside the window.

I sigh, utterly relaxed, completely, ridiculously happy, and Gray runs his hands through my hair. I rest my head under his neck and it fits just right. His other arm's around my waist, pinning me tight against him. Like he never wants to let me go.

We talk about it a little bit. I admit at first it hurt, but when I relaxed it felt good. I lift my head up and we both glance over at the clock.

"You lasted almost five minutes," I point out, and Gray winces.

"I was hoping you wouldn't notice that," he says.

"That's not good?" I ask, and he laughs.

"No," he says. "It's pathetic. But it took every ounce of mental discipline to go that long."

Gray promises me sex only gets better, and we agree we'd like to practice. He tells me, speaking of practice, he can set up a training schedule. And now he rambles.

He informs me every morning will begin with some calisthenics followed by sex. Then we'll eat a breakfast rich in carbohydrates to maintain energy, followed by sex. In the evening, there'll be some warm-up stretches followed by sex. Then a cooldown followed by more sex. Then ice cream, preferably chocolate. Then sleep to rest up for morning practice.

I brush my lips across his warm shoulder. "I'm glad to see you're a normal healthy male."

* * * * *

*Gray's content to spend the next day in bed,* but the sun's bright and beckoning me to play outside. When he gets out of the bathroom, I announce I found a hiking trail in downtown Los Angeles.

"The woman at the front desk recommended it," I say.

He tells me I'm nuts.

"People don't walk in L.A., Dylan. Let alone hike," he says.

I'm determined to try, so we drive to west L.A. and north of Hollywood Boulevard, carved through the hills, is a park called Runyon Canyon. We find parking on Vista Street and climb the steep pavement to the entrance. People are coming and going in droves to enjoy the beautiful day. Gray gapes at all the chiseled, greased-up bodies that surround us. I'm pretty sure we're the only ones there wearing T-shirts.

"I think you have to be a supermodel to use the park," he says, but I'm too ecstatic to see dogs scampering everywhere to notice all the beautiful people.

We hike up a gravel trail that slowly ascends over the city. We stop and look out at a mirage of skyscrapers spread out in a smoggy skyline below. Gray points out the cluster of buildings that make up South Central and Century City and Westwood. When we reach the top of the trail we have views of the multimillion-dollar homes packed tightly together in the Hollywood Hills, and I photograph the Hollywood sign, perched on top of the mountain like a constant spotlight. I turn to start the climb back down, but Gray grabs my arm. He points to an open gate on the other side of the trailhead, and we walk through it to discover we're standing at the edge of Mulholland Drive.

Gray tells me Mulholland is one of the most famous streets in Los Angeles, known for its steep winding turns over the hills, connecting the valley and downtown.

"We can drive down it tonight," he assures me. "It has the best views of the city." He turns to head back into the park, but I grab his shirt.

"Let's walk down it right now," I say.

We stand at the edge of the curving road and watch cars take the sharp turns too fast. He shakes his head and tells me he's driven down Mulholland lots of times, but he's never seen a pedestrian attempt to walk down it.

"Why not?" Just as I ask this, a Mercedes barrels around the corner and nearly takes out my knee. I jump back, and instead of slowing down, the driver honks and sticks his head out the window.

"Lay off the crack," he yells at us.

Gray nods to the guy. "Thank you," he shouts, and waves at him. I wave too, with a wide grin.

"We have every right to use this road," I insist as another car comes within inches of hitting us.

Gray throws his arms up in defeat because he knows my crazy ideas will always win out over his rational ones. He offers to hold my camera, and as I follow behind him the road descends so quickly that we start to run. We're sprinting and cars are nearly grazing our sides and I can't stop laughing because I think we're the only people nuts enough to attempt this (or I'm getting high off of car fumes).

We soon discover why running down Mulholland is madness. Not only are there no sidewalks, but there's no shoulder next to the road, so walking it is about as safe as strolling straight into oncoming traffic.

When we come to a lookout spot on the side of the street, we stop to catch our breath. Gray points out the 101 Highway below us, packed with a steady stream of cars, and the Hollywood Bowl in the distance, a famous outdoor music venue where he's seen a few bands. He grabs my arm and we're running again and waving at tour buses and cars as they pass. I'm getting a cramp in my side from sprinting and laughing at the same time. Gray says we still have miles to go.

We find a steady pace and I start singing the lyrics to "Like a Rolling Stone," and Gray joins in. My leg muscles start to burn and I can feel sweat dripping down my chest. Finally Mulholland ends only to connect to Cahuenga Boulevard. Cahuenga is a straight shot, but it runs parallel to the 101 Highway and cars take it just as fast. We stay close to the edge, but there's still no sidewalk. Cars are flying past us at eighty miles an hour and I'm screaming and Gray turns to ask if I'm okay but I'm laughing too hard to answer him.

A highway ramp suddenly merges with the road and we have to cross it to get to the other side. People refuse to slow down for two insane pedestrians trying to use a freeway for their afternoon run. When there's a second break, Gray and I dive forward and sprint for our lives to make it to the other side.

We continue to run down Cahuenga and finally a shoulder appears along the road. We pass the Hollywood Bowl entrance. We're sheltered under the shade of eucalyptus trees, and Gray slows down and tells me to break the leaves open and smell them. We each grab a handful of leaves and inhale their cool, sweet scent. It's a nice relief from breathing in so much engine exhaust.

We pick up our pace again and pass Franklin Street and run alongside lanes of cars stuck in bumper-to-bumper traffic. We hear impatient tires screech and horns honk. Seeing all these people confined in those closed, tight spaces on such a gorgeous, sunny day makes me feel free, and I think they're the crazy ones and wonder if their looks are something closer to jealousy than surprise.

When we get close to Hollywood Boulevard, there's finally a sidewalk. I sprint with all the energy I have left and Gray races me to the finish line. We dodge tourists on the sidewalk. I scream that I think I see Cher up ahead and Gray yells that he just saw Alec Baldwin down the street, and people are turning their heads to look. When we make it to Hollywood Boulevard, we're both flushed and covered in sweat.

We finally stop running and buy some bottled waters and weave through tourists. We pass people dressed up like Captain Jack Sparrow and Spider-Man and the Hulk and I stop to take pictures with every one of them. We get sandwiches for lunch and then Gray pulls me into a music store and we spend hours looking through more CDs than I've ever seen in my life.

I ask Gray why he loves music so much. He looks at me and his eyes are as bright as the sky and his face is pink and his hair's a mess and I'm positive he's the most beautiful person in Los Angeles. He grabs a few strands of loose hair around my face and tries to wind them back into my ponytail. My stomach flips from his touch, and from the way he's looking at me I know what he's thinking about. Sex. It's probably the hundredth time he's thought about it today, because the kid will not stop glowing. I can't help thinking about it either. How it felt last night. And earlier this morning. And again, later this morning. Hopefully we'll be having it again soon, but maybe after a shower.

"Gray," I say, and he blinks back to reality. I smile at him. "Stop thinking about sex and answer my question." He blushes and tells me sex is the furthest thing from his mind.

"Right," I say. "I know when your mind's in the gutter."

He shrugs and concentrates on my question. He tells me it's hard to explain.

"Music is life-changing," he says. I tell him to give me an example.

He scrolls through some albums. He tells me music can change your mood instantly. It can make memories feel present and any dream seem tangible.

"I'm convinced people like Bob Dylan and the Beatles and Paul Simon are magicians," he says. He tells me that one song has the power to time warp you to the past. Transport you to the future. Wake up the dead. Put you under a spell. And you come out of it transfixed.

He pulls a U2 album out of the rack and points to the playlist.

"I can have the worst day of my life and all I have to do is play one track and it has the power to shut out every negative thought in my mind, every worry, every frustration. Music can transform you," he says. "It can make you new again. It's like medicine."

He ends up buying five CDs from the five-dollar bin and I buy a collection of love songs on sale for two dollars. We walk outside and I set my CD on the ground in front of the music store and Gray asks me what I'm doing. I grab his hand and we cross the street and sit on a bench. We watch people saunter by and glance at the CD. A woman with two kids stops to examine it but she doesn't pick it up. Finally, a man walking by himself bends down and picks it up. He's wearing a business suit and he looks tired and his gray hair's a tangled mess. He looks at the CD and glances around. He shrugs and puts it in his bag. I smile and tell Gray maybe he needs to listen to it. Maybe it will be life-changing for him.

We walk back to the car and drive to In-N-Out for dinner. We lift up the back of Gray's hatchback and sit on the edge so we can eat with the sunlight pouring in and listen to music. We're sunburned and sore from running, and we take turns rubbing each other's calves and shins. We head back to the hotel, where Gray's ready to settle in for the night because he knows what's in store. Before I have to ask if he's having a good time he tells me today has been the greatest day of his life.

## Gray

*I do the "I just got laid," walk for days* after our trip to Los Angeles. It's more like a strut. It's pretty obvious when you're doing it. Your mind is clouded in a euphoric high. Your head is held at an angle twenty degrees higher than normal. There's a continual smart-ass grin on your face. Your eyes twinkle, literally, as if stardust fell inside them. You walk taller. Prouder. Your back is held straighter. Shoulders wider. You know you're hot. It's been proven. You had sex.

So, what do I think while I'm in this mind-set? Mostly this: When will I have sex again?

The best part of all: Nothing can bring you down. No words can harm you. No one can annoy you. This is a bullet-proof state of mind. You're cocky and confident, as if the world should lay down a red carpet under your feet and reporters should stand in line to ask, "What's your secret? Why did she pick you?"

The world is set right again. Sexual healing. I now understand why Marvin Gaye's song is so good.

# ||| FIRST LIVE |||

## Gray

*One week left until Dylan's leaving* but I deny it to myself because it's easier than facing circumstances I would never choose and can't avoid.

I could dwell on the fact that she's leaving and let myself feel sick about it. Do I start to slowly distance myself from her now? I mean, what's the point of falling more in love with Dylan every day when I know it has to come to an end? Why set myself up for that kind of pain? Haven't I had enough pain in my life?

But if I knew Amanda was going to die, would I have distanced myself from her to make it easier? That's insane. I would have spent as much time with her as possible. Documented everything. Appreciated every moment. Told her how amazing she was, how much I loved her, how much she'd added to my life. Because if you're lucky enough to have people in your life that make you happy, that inspire you, that move you, you need to devour each moment you have together because you never know how many of those moments you have left. These people are sacred.

So, we spend every possible waking, sleeping, breathing minute together. I leave her only to go to work. We finish painting projects for her Aunt Diane-Dan. We take hikes around the city.

I don't mind, because usually both activities end with a shower, which ends with sex. And the sex is life-changing. Mind-altering. It consumes my thoughts. The more I have it, the more I need it. And I'm getting better at it. I've figured out ways to touch Dylan that make her legs shake. Her back arch. Her breaths come out in gasps, her voice in groans. It's true what they say, sex only gets better. And no one's ever told me that it's way more satisfying to get a girl off than to get off yourself. I'm glad I figured that one out on my own.

I've been avoiding my house. My parents have treated my Mighty Squall (as Dylan and I refer to it) as though that's all it was, just a wild, unexpected storm front that blew through our lives and tossed things around but it's passed now. Forgotten. Just a freak incident. Our lives have settled back into a safe avoidance routine. And it really pisses me off that in the last few days our family talks have contained all the love and warmth of newspaper headlines with no story attached. Quick. To the point. Sufficiently informative, but lacking any depth. And this used to be enough. But someone's taught me to expect more out of people and never to settle.

✳ ✳ ✳ ✳ ✳

*It's Saturday afternoon and my mom and dad* are sitting in the family room to escape the heat. I'm leaving to take Dylan on a hike to Silly Mountain, a trail outside Phoenix that I'm surprised she never discovered on her own. My dad gives me this strange look when I walk in the room. Like he's actually happy to see me. Like for once he has something to say to me beyond a weather forecast or to inform me of his next business trip.

He tells me Coach Clark called him yesterday to discuss the scholarship. My dad clears his throat and he looks surprised.

"He told me you already accepted the offer."

I nod. I did accept it. I have a list of reasons ready to fire out. I'm an adult. They can't stop me. I don't need their money. I'll be fine. It's a free education. It's a free country. It's *my life*. They should lead by example and get on with their own lives.

But he doesn't argue with me.

I see relief pass over his eyes. And something else. Something strange. Then I realize he's happy. He's the happiest I've seen him since Amanda died.

"You want me to play?" I ask.

He tells me of course he wants me to play. He stands up and walks over to me and presses his hand on my shoulder. He tells me I made the right decision and he's proud of me for taking the initiative. I stare at him, our eyes level with each other.

"Really?" I ask.

"You were right. You can't pass this up."

I nod and I glance at my mom, who's staring at the floor, silent.

"It looks like I'll be adding Albuquerque to my travel plans this spring," he says. "There's one more thing, Gray." He tells me he's also been thinking about seeing a counselor. He just never imagined I'd be willing to go through with it, he admits. He's shocked that I was the first one to bring it up.

I shrug. It's amazing how far you're willing to go when someone believes in you. He assures me, again, that he wants me to play baseball. Nothing would make him and my mom more proud.

"Before you leave for school," he says, "I made a few appointments for us all to meet with a family therapist."

I tell him I think that's great. I look at my mom again and her hands are folded in her lap and she gives me a slow nod. She sighs and her breath is so heavy, so toiling. She's still feeling the most pain. She's the most damaged. After Amanda died, she curled in on herself, like the burnt corners of paper. She shriveled and became half the person she used to be. I was worried she'd slowly curl up all together and smother herself in darkness.

Tears roll down her cheeks and a shaky breath escapes her lips. It makes my heart ache to see her so wounded. I wish I could make the pain stop. You'd think time would help her to heal, but I know grieving happens in waves and feelings get recycled. One day you wake up with more energy and the heavy cloud of sadness lifts off your face and you attempt to rejoin civilization, but then you're suddenly reminded. It can be as simple as hearing a song on the radio or seeing a movie title or stumbling upon an old photograph—the memory kicks you right in the hollow spot of your heart and the relapse of pain rushes back like a flood. The cycle's relentless and exhausting and can be more discouraging than it's worth, because it seems like every time life kicks you back down, you fall a little bit harder, and pretty soon the bruises pile up and you're too tired to get up and try again. So eventually, you stop trying at all. That's what's happened to my mom.

She stands up and walks over to me and she practically falls into my arms. I'm stunned, and I just wrap my arms around her skinny, shaking frame and hold her tight as she cries into my T-shirt.

"I'm so sorry, Gray," she says, and she chokes on her words because she's crying so hard. "I haven't been there for you. But I love you so much," she says. "I hope you know that."

I nod and tell her I know. I tell her I love her.

"I hope you can forgive me," she says through a sob.

I swallow and I tell her of course I forgive her. I tell her I was never, ever angry with her.

"And I'm not leaving," I say. "I'm just going to school. I'll always be here, I promise."

We all cry. And for the first time since Amanda's death, it

feels healing. Not suffocating. Not distressing. Not blinding with heartache. This time it's cleansing. Awakening. A small step forward.

✳ ✳ ✳ ✳ ✳

*I suck it up and call Brandon Stack,* my old high school best friend, because if I'm going to seriously commit to making one hell of a comeback, I need all the training I can get. I tell him the news and he's so happy for me. He compliments me, saying what a great team I'm signing with. He says Coach Clark is the best in the conference. We talk for an hour. He tells me he'd love to work out before I leave town. He says that he's still training with some of the team and I'm welcome to join him. I tell him I'd like that. He says it's great to hear from me again. And just like that I have a friend back.

I thought he'd be mad and I thought he'd remind me that I've ignored him for almost a year, hold it against me and hold his friendship at arm's length because that's what I did to him. But he doesn't. I was the one holding him away. And I thought he got so cocky, so self-absorbed. But I was the self-absorbed one. My life was tragic, my future shards, while his life was spread out before him past a golden archway. I was too beat up to have the energy to care about anyone, because all I could do was breathe. Some nights I was amazed to get to sleep without sleeping pills.

As I drive to Dylan's, I feel dizzy trying to wrap my mind around all the changes happening in my life. I'm trying to accept that it's okay to be happy. I shouldn't feel guilty for being excited about life.

Now there's only one person who will make it perfect, who will frame my new life and hold it together, in place, so I can hang it up for everyone to admire.

She's changed my life. And she's leaving in four days. When your world's become one person, how do you prepare to let her go? How do you get over someone you know you'll never forget? There's only one option. I *won't* let her go. I'll convince Dylan to move to New Mexico with me.

# Ⅲ First Enjoy It Ⅲ

## Gray

*We've been having sex all morning,* but I still can't last longer than eight fricking minutes and Dylan doesn't care but I do and I'm determined to stretch it out so she can enjoy it. And I love a challenge.

I shut my eyes and try to focus on baseball stats. It's all about mental toughness, Gray. List the starting lineup for the Arizona Diamondbacks. First base: Adam LaRoche. Second base: Kelly Johnson. Third base: Mark Reynolds.

I gasp. I'm getting close. No, no, I can keep going. Where did I leave off? Third base. No. Shit. Shortstop. Speaking of shortstop. Don't let it be short. Make it last. Okay, forget shortstop. Catcher: Miguel Montero. Left field: Gerardo Parra. Center field: Chris Young. Right field: Justin Upton.

Three more minutes. Come on, put your game face on, Gray. You can do it. Last three more minutes. Be a man. It's game time.

"Wait, Dylan, we need to slow down."

"Why?"

"I'm trying to last."

She leans her damp cheek against mine and her hot breath is

in my ear. "Think about the ugliest male teacher you've ever had," she tells me, and then she licks my ear.

I laugh. Okay, brilliant idea. Ugly teachers . . . that's easy. Mr. Frederickson. Fifth grade. *Ugh*. It is not possible to have a beer gut that big and still be able to stand up straight. His three alternating polo shirts always had grease stains. Everywhere. And who can forget the pit stains? And his breath? *Lethal*. It could be used to torture terror suspects. I didn't raise my hand once that entire year in fear he'd come over and blast me with breath so bad it was probably flammable.

This is good. This is working.

Eighth grade. Mrs. Kelly, English teacher. She never wore a bra and she was always nipping out.

Uh, I'm getting close.

No! Make a list. Any list. List places to take Dylan before she leaves. Hiking. Hiking is good. But it's so hot. Too hot.

"I'm close," I breathe.

Hiking. We're hiking. Where, where the hell are we hiking?

"Hiking," I moan.

"What?"

"Nothing!"

We're at Sunset Crater National Park. Black ash. Active volcanoes. Red sand. Lava flows. Fissures. Eruptions. Spilling. Pouring. I'm sinking. No! Not yet. One more minute.

Cold days. Freezing cold. Falling through ice. Ice smoothies. Icies. 7-Eleven. Swiss Cake Rolls. Little Debbie. Oatmeal Cream Pies. Creamy, sweet goodness.

I can't hold it anymore. So I let it go. My fingers dig into her hips. My toes curl and then they release. I'm sweating and shaking and done and Dylan isn't even close and I know that. I take a long, deep breath and I swear I'm floating.

"Give me ten minutes. I can go again," I say. I swing her over on her back so I can play with her, but she leans away from me and says it's time for a cooldown. She grabs a glass of water off my nightstand and takes a long swig. She hands it to me and I gulp down the rest, but it takes a few seconds because I'm panting. My sheets are damp. Blankets have been kicked off hours ago. Pillows are thrown askew. Condom wrappers litter the carpeting. It smells like sex everywhere, hot, steamy skin and salt and bleach. It's my idea of heaven.

My forehead's wet. Dylan's legs are sticky. Our bodies are stuck to each other. I have to peel my arm off of hers like tape. Our chests are clammy and wet and suctioned together and I love it. She wraps her calf around my thigh and I rest my head on her chest and grin because her heart's hammering as hard as mine and her breaths are just as sharp. I lean up on my elbow and stare into her eyes, inches from mine.

"This is intense," I tell her, my breath still shaky.

"It's a good way to spend the afternoon," she says.

I nod enthusiastically, my eyes are still on hers, and all these feelings are spilling out of my mind and pouring through my veins. My body is shifting into pieces and it feels like my lungs are in my throat and my brain's in my chest and my heart's in my hands and my hands are on fire.

"It's too much," I finally say. I wave my hand over the open space between our bodies. "It's too perfect." She presses her hand down on the mattress.

"It's all right," she says. "I think it's a little hard, personally."

I roll my eyes. "Not the mattress. You and me. I feel like I've known you my whole my life. I mean, shouldn't sex be a little more awkward than this?" I point out how sweaty and naked and perfectly at ease we are together.

She reminds me what a nervous wreck I was the first time. She says I looked ready to pee my pants, but it was adorable.

I narrow my eyes. "Weren't you scared?" I ask. She shakes her head.

"No," she says. "I always knew we'd be perfect." As usual, her confidence baffles me. I trace the smooth ridge of her collarbone. I tell Dylan I've hooked up with other girls. I've never had sex with them, but it came close a few times. And they would get so shy. So self-conscious. It made me inhibited because we were always holding back. Giving just enough because we didn't want to look slutty and taking just enough because we didn't want to seem greedy. It's like we were skating, moving too slow and stiffly, overly careful that we'd fall and make fools out of ourselves or, the worst fear of all, not live up to each other's expectations. And I thought that was *normal*.

But with Dylan, sex has been like every other part of our relationship. Intense and exhilarating and effortless.

Dylan runs her fingers through my hair.

"Life's too short to be bashful," she says. "We're all just human and far from perfect, so why not enjoy it?"

"Not many people are that self-assured," I remind her.

She shrugs and says who cares what other people think? If you're lucky enough to fall in love with someone, then forget about your imperfections. Because in their eyes, you're perfect. You won't get anywhere in life until you let go of your stupid ego.

"What do you think about during sex?" I ask, because I'm curious.

She stares up at the ceiling and says Ashton Kutcher.

"What?" I say, and she rolls her eyes and lightly bats me on the head.

"I think about you, Gray," she says. She thinks about how lucky she is to be with me and she just wants to savor every second of it, and I'm amazed because that's exactly how I feel about her and maybe when you take yourself out of the equation and let yourself be there for someone else, you lose sight of your insecurities. I take a deep breath.

"Maybe you should come to New Mexico with me," I hint for the first time.

Dylan looks back at me and there's a weighted silence and a seriousness to her eyes that scares me, so I try to make light of it.

"We have a lot more practice days left on my training schedule," I inform her.

She cracks a laugh and it hurts a little because even though I'm skipping around the real reason why I want her to come with me, I'm still serious.

"You don't need any more practice," she says. "You're a natural." Then her eyes turn serious and she stares at me. "How am I?" she asks, and her words surprise me. She's never asked me a question like this before. She's never once asked me if I thought she was pretty or smart or why I like her—things my past girlfriends would always bug me about. Dylan doesn't need other people's validation to know how amazing she is. But she looks curious now. I stare at her face, golden against the white sheets. Sex with her is numbing and intoxicating. Something like a narcotic mixed with a miracle. I tell her it's indescribable.

She tells me to try.

I lean back on the bed and do my best to explain it.

"Sometimes it's a rush, like skydiving, and other times it's just a smooth ride, like floating in the middle of a calm lake. It's like standing next to a hot fire that's shooting sparks, or walking on the sun and then rolling in the snow. It's like plate tectonics and hailstorms and lightning and earthquakes and hurricane-force winds all happening at once but then everything suddenly stops moving and your mind draws a blank and everything's really peaceful. It's like your mind explodes and all that's left inside your body is heat." I cut myself off because I'm rambling and I turn to look at her and she's just staring at me with this surprised look on her face.

"What?" I ask.

She blinks at me. "You said you couldn't write poetry," she said. I smile. I just needed inspiration. I needed to start living again to find writing material.

She leans back on her arm.

"I can make you feel like that?" she asks, and I nod. She looks at me and congratulates me and I ask her for what.

"For finally letting down all your walls," she says, and I smile and she's right and all this sex talk has made me ready to go again.

# ⅠⅠⅠ First Dream ⅠⅠⅠ

## Dylan

*Gray and I take Boba for a walk in the late afternoon* at the park with the fountain and the circular path. There's plenty of shade available to keep Boba from going into cardiac arrest.

Gray tells me he's already packing for Albuquerque. He says he called Brandon and he's going to start practicing with his team tomorrow and every day before he leaves for school. He's starting to look into fall classes. My heart is soaring for him. A few months ago his life was shattered glass. His future a cage. Today, it's a clear blue sky. It's a solid path set out before him as wide as the desert horizon. He's finally stepping into a world that always felt out of reach. He deserves it more than anyone.

I tell him I'm so excited for him, and Gray turns to look at me and he broadens his shoulders and raises his chin.

"I want you to come with me," he says. It's not a question; it's a statement, as if he has no doubt I'll say yes. But instead of leaping at the offer, my body wants to sink. I have to make an effort to hold myself up.

I want to look away, but his eyes are fixed stubbornly on mine. This is it. We can't tiptoe around the issue. We can't make light of it anymore. There isn't time. I'm leaving in two days.

I don't answer him; I just keep walking. Stalling. I can sense him starting to panic. Silence, for me, is usually a bad sign.

"This isn't a spontaneous idea," he says. "I've thought about it every day since Coach Clark made me the offer."

Gray maps out our future together. He tells me I can move with him next month, find a part-time job, work on my photography, maybe take a few classes.

I'm quiet and Gray thinks I'm considering the offer. He promises I'll love Albuquerque. It's in a canyon and it's surrounded with stacks of red rocks, deserts, and mountains. It's a photographer's paradise. There are hiking trails everywhere.

"We can discover it together," he says. I smile at him, but it's forced. I feel it stop short of my eyes.

"We could get a puppy," he says, just to entice me. He lists breeds. A Great Dane, a Weimaraner, a chocolate Lab, one of those goldendoodle things, he doesn't care. His words make tears splinter the back of my eyes. The more he talks, the harder my chest aches, because I know I have to let him down.

"We could adopt Boba," he says. "The world's smelliest mammal. It would be my housewarming gift," he offers. "Best of all," he reminds me, "I'll be there."

For the first time in my life, I'm speechless. He's offering me his future. But that's the problem. It's *his* life, it isn't mine. I could never follow someone else's path. Can't he see that? Doesn't he understand? I've been waiting seventeen years to finally strike out on my own.

When there's more silence, Gray keeps rambling, because he'd rather talk than hear an answer he can't accept. He lists the reasons why he wants me there, needs me there. He lists off the fun things we can do.

"Think of all the road trips we can take," he says. "Utah, the Grand Canyon, Colorado, Vegas . . ."

He tells me we can get married. I stop walking and stare at him.

"You're joking."

"I'm serious," he demands. "I love you. Don't you get it? You're the one. We're meant for each other. I could spend every day with you. I could build that house we designed on Camelback. Well, if I was a millionaire," he adds.

I can barely swallow.

He tells me this is it. It's what people wait their entire lives to find and we're lucky enough to experience it. He tells me he doesn't want to pass this up just because of bad timing. He says we can make our own timing. We can be in charge of time.

"Gray—"

"If you want to marry me, I'll ask you right now. Or, we can look at rings first, whatever you want."

"Are you seriously proposing to me?" I ask. Please say no. For the love of God and sanity and my emotional well-being, please say no.

He holds his head up high and tells me, yes, he is. He fixes his eyes intensely on mine.

"Dylan, will you marry me?" he asks.

I can only stare at him. My legs are frozen with shock. Boba yanks on the leash and nearly pulls my arm out of its socket. He starts dragging me down the sidewalk like he's humiliated for Gray. I'm surprised that instead of feeling happy or amazed or even panicked, more than anything, I'm angry. Furious.

"You're being ridiculous," I say. I tell him he's scared for all the changes that are about to happen and he's grasping for something constant to hold on to.

He argues it isn't true. He tells me he loves me and I'm the most important thing in the world to him. His voice cracks.

"I don't want to lose you," he says.

I stop because I finally know what I need to say.

"Gray, I'm not yours to lose."

# Gray

*I watch her as the words slowly sink in.*

Her eyes are sad and serious, brimming with tears, eyes I have never seen until this moment. It's breathtaking to see pain behind them. She always saved her sadness. She kept it in. She let me be sad this summer; she let me be angry and hurt and lonely and depressed. Her eyes silence me. Nothing is more distressing than a sad angel. I know what her answer is.

"You're not even going to think about it?" I ask. I'm not desperate, I want to add. I'm not trying to hold on to Dylan just because I can't live without her. All I know is, I'm convinced I want her more than anything. So, my reasoning is simple. It makes perfect sense for her to join me.

"Of course I've thought about it," she says. "And it probably all sounds perfect to you. But I need to get to know myself first, Gray. I need to be complete with who I am before I try to be there for someone else."

I feel like the sky's falling down around me. My forehead creases with confusion. "So I'm not enough?" I argue.

This question makes the tears stream down her face.

She tells me she wants to travel. She wants to see the world. She tells me she just broke the surface this summer. She came down here to start her journey, and this is just the beginning. She says she didn't come down here to fall in love.

"But you *did*," I remind her, and she winces as if my words hurt. Sometimes the simplest words cut the deepest if they're aimed right.

"I love you," she says. "But that doesn't mean I'm ready to

give up my life for you. I don't want to pull over and park right now. I want to see places, Gray. I want to live *my* life. You're asking me to give up who I am. If I move with you, I'll just be living your life. Your dream. I'll regret the things you're going to hold me back from doing, and then I'll probably blame you. And that's not fair to either of us."

My brain twists with anger to hear the truth. I have to make an effort to breathe. I try to make sense of her logic. And sadly, right now she's the logical one. I'm crazy. Crazy for her.

"Where are you going to go?" I ask.

She tells me after her cousin's wedding she's heading out west. She wants to spend some time in California.

"I had a phone interview with a coffee shop in Shasta City," she says. "They offered me the job. They said I can start next month."

She has the nerve to smile, and it only fuels my anger.

"When did you decide all this?" I demand to know.

"I've known for a few days," she says. "I started looking after you told me you accepted the offer from New Mexico."

She keeps walking. She tells me she wants to live on the side of a mountain. Then she wants to live on the coast. Someday she wants to live in a huge city where she can ride a train to work and live in a studio downtown with creaky hardwood floors and old, drafty windows. She wants to learn Spanish and travel in Central America. She wants to get out of the States and spend a summer in Italy. She wants to backpack up the east coast of Australia. She isn't ready to give up her future.

My heart sinks, and my shoulders sink, and my head and my neck and my life. Of course this is what she needs to do. Why did I have to fall in love with a girl as easy to tag down as the wind? I can't ask her to sit around a college town for me. She would hate it. And she's right. She would resent me for crippling her dreams.

Tears well up in my eyes, and I quickly blink them away.

We continue down the path and Boba pants between us. I'm walking but I feel like I'm wading through water. Every step takes effort. We're both silent. What do you say when you're not enough to make someone stay? What do you do when you meet the love of your life and realize it's all about timing? How do you accept that no matter how perfect you are for each other, circumstances get in the way? How do you compete with that kind of fate?

# ⏐⏐⏐ FIRST BELIEVE ⏐⏐⏐

## Dylan

*I left this morning.*

Last night Gray stayed up making me a going-away present. Ten mixes. He admitted it was a little extreme. He made two or three, then figured he might as well round it off with five. He told me that after he burned five CDs, he realized he didn't make me anything with rap. I couldn't be deprived of at least one hip-hop CD. So, one led to a few more. He realized he didn't burn any Led Zeppelin, any Lenny Kravitz. Not one Jimi Hendrix song. Then, he almost forgot to make me the Ultimate Road Trip Mix. How can I possibly drive without Tom Petty, the Eagles, Bruce Springsteen, and John Mellencamp? What kind of rustic road trip scenery can go unaccompanied by these voices leading me along, without "American Girl," "Easy Feeling," "Born to Run," and "Jack and Diane"? It's like watching a movie with no soundtrack, he said.

All of the CDs were labeled using our summer memories: *Running down Mulholland*, *Santa Monica*, and *Camelback Mountain*. One mix was titled *Walking with Boba* (obviously featuring slower songs). Gray informed me the most difficult and crucial element to making a mix is to choose its title, since it sets the mood for the entire compilation.

The last mix he made has the word *love* in every song. It's my favorite one.

I gave Gray a scrapbook to give to his dad. It's a coffee table book of collected photography. It captures our entire summer together. It's frozen memories: shots of our hikes around Phoenix, pictures of cactuses, shots of motorcycles parked along the curb of Mill Avenue, their chrome chests jutting in the sun, shots of Sedona, even a few of Los Angeles. I included the photograph of the two geckos talking in the sun. I love that picture. It's the day we met. Strange to think that two geckos brought us together.

I made Gray a gift, something thin and rectangular that I wrapped in newspaper. I told him to open it after I left. He gave me a CD case to strap on my visor with the ten mixes inside. He said he hoped Pickle would make it for two thousand miles of freeway driving. He told me to stay in the right lane unless I wanted to instigate road rage. Good advice.

We said goodbye in the morning, early, when the sun was still low in a mauve-colored sky. The air was unseasonably cool. He wore a jacket. It was the first time I'd ever seen Gray in a coat. It already made him feel distant. We both hate goodbyes, so we made it quick, like ripping off a sticky bandage or pulling a sliver from our skin.

He wrapped his arms around me and held me so close our ribs were connecting. He kept breathing me in. I could feel my heart rise and sink, rise and sink with every breath.

I couldn't stop the tears spilling from my eyes. He swept them away with his fingers. I knew saying goodbye would be hard, but I never knew it could physically *hurt*, as though a rope were strangling my heart.

I told Gray I loved him over and over. He told me he loved me. He said I changed his life. I couldn't put into words how much he changed mine. But then he said something that wasn't fair. He said if I really loved him, I wouldn't leave him.

"You're leaving too," I reminded him. I said we both needed to leave in order to live.

"I want to see you again" is all he said.

I promised him he would.

He told me he loved me again. He's like one of those cactuses we saw hiking this summer. His center is finally exposed.

I told Gray to keep on loving. To love as many people as he could. I promised it would come back to him if he did. He shook his head. He told me he could only love me, and it scared me because I knew he meant it.

"I'm not your only love, Gray," I insisted. "I'm just your first love."

## Gray

*I'm sitting in my room staring at cardboard boxes* stuffed with things I don't want. Crap I don't need. All I want is you. U2 nailed it.

I can still see Dylan's car driving away, the rusty orange station wagon growing tinier in the distance like a fading sunset. I can still feel her tears on my fingers. They were hot to my touch, like desert rain.

This fucking hurts. Why does loving someone have to fucking *hurt?*

I don't know when I'll see Dylan again. She doesn't use any online networks. She doesn't have a profile. She's the only person I've ever met my age that doesn't own a cell phone. Things with wires, with signals, with connections, don't fit her. Anything that has a definite place, with an end and a beginning, doesn't suit her.

She can't be tied down. It's cruel that what I love most about Dylan is the very reason why I can't have her.

I stare down at the photography book she made for my dad, just like she said she would. Dylan always follows through with what she says. It's a little scary sometimes. I know he'll think it's bizarre that a girl he's never met is giving him a glimpse of the world through her eyes. But what can I say? That's just Dylan.

I pick up the gift she gave me and tear through the wrapping. Inside is a framed poem. The memory of the title makes me smile.

"Ode to the Mighty Green Ones."

The poem we wrote together when we first met. On the side of the poem is a photograph taped to the paper, from our hiking trip. It's a single, saguaro cactus standing proud in the desert sun. Its arms are stretched out like it's embracing the air and trying to touch the sky. I read the words and even though I wrote half of the poem, every sentence reminds me of her:

> *My Phoenix cactus*
> *My tall saguaro tower*
> *Strong and independent*
> *Silent and wise*
> *You live to be two hundred*
> *But you are too prickly*
> *If I fell on you*
> *My body would be contaminated*
> *With needle-point stab wounds*
> *As if a crazy old woman*
> *Tried to kill me by using*
> *Her sewing needles*
> *But I admire your arms*
> *Stretched out in the wind*

*On more arms stretched out*
*On more arms stretched out*
*On more*
*And I love arms*
*But yours are too prickly*
*Because if you hugged me*
*I'd die in your embrace*
*Literally*
*I will always adore you*
*From a distance*
*And want to water you*
*But you don't need me*
*Is that why I'm fond of you?*

She's gone.

And it feels like my heart is drained of something solid. Empty. But, she was right. She never belonged to me. Now one thought gives me hope.

I told her I wanted to see her again. And she promised me I would.

# ||| FIRST GROW |||

## One Month Later

## Gray

*Hey, God, did I do something to piss you off?* Because I'm starting to think you enjoy twisting the knife in my heart every chance you get. If too much happiness dares to encroach on my life, does some siren go off up there? Uh-oh, Gray's too happy right now. We can't have that. Time to shit all over his life again.

Apparently I'm not cut out for happiness. Not my destiny, I guess.

Those were the majority of my thoughts as I drove east to New Mexico. The rest of the time I tried to block out my mind with Rage Against the Machine and Ludacris and Limp Bizkit—people that share my current hostility toward life, and beats that are loud enough to keep me awake during the dozing-off points on boring stretches of highway.

I filled up my hatchback with the most crucial essentials: baseball glove, stereo, music, guitar, and computer. I packed a few bags of clothes. I thought about stealing Dylan's photography book from my dad and bringing it with me. Not because I want vivid memories of every moment we had together so I can torture myself with daily reminders. But it has a picture of her inside, the only one I have access to. It's a picture I took in Phoenix: She's standing in between Boba and this iron statue of a man pointing, and she's pretending to be the person he's pointing at. She's trying to be funny, but she looks gorgeous with the sun hitting her hair so it's shining, and it captures her wide smile and her slender body from head to toe.

I moved into a four-bedroom house on campus, a ten-minute walk from the Tow Diem Facility, where the baseball team weight trains. It's also close to Lobo Field, our main practice field. We play our season games at the Isotopes Park, a stadium that UNM shares with a triple-A baseball league in Albuquerque.

My three roommates, Miles, Todd, and Mark (Mark's nickname is Bubba), are all baseball players. Todd and Bubba have girlfriends, who are always over, pestering them to do things or hang out or study, and the guys act like they can't be bothered. Miles desperately wants a girlfriend and he's the one who's single. It always seems to work that way.

I just like living with people who move and talk and make noise. It's a nice change.

My room's tucked up on the third floor and has white walls that smell freshly painted, and it's furnished but in an old-school way, as if the person before me had a thing for antiques. I don't really care. It's a fresh start with no memories attached, and that's all I need. I have a full-size bed and a wood desk that's barely big enough for my legs to fit underneath. There's a dresser in the corner of the room with a mirror over it, which I take down and replace with a Bob Dylan concert poster Amanda bought me. I stuff Dylan's framed poem in the bottom drawer of my nightstand. I set my guitar case against the wall next to the door. It only takes an hour to unpack my life.

My favorite part of my room is a door leading out to a fire escape. Whoever designed it figured there might as well be a sitting area in case you need to catch your breath while you're dodging a burning building. So I've inherited a private balcony that faces southwest over rooftops sprawled out below. It's an oasis from the rest of the world. It's a place I can just be alone, which I need more than the average person. I crave space. It charges my batteries. It helps me breathe. Being around people can be so exhausting, because most of them love to take and barely know how to give. Except for a rare few.

My body is sore and tight from muscles that haven't been used in more than a year. Coach Clark wasn't kidding about his training intensity. He meets with me almost every day to make sure I'm lifting, doing squats, running, jump-roping, throwing, swinging. To make sure I'm paying for taking an extended vacation. But I like the physical pain. It reminds me that I'm finally focused on the future and on a goal I have some control over. And the endorphins give me this natural high. Like I'm immortal. Like nothing can hurt me. Kind of like sex. But not nearly as good.

I'm the new kid on the team, and so far everyone's welcomed me in like a brother. Todd's the only person who's brought up Amanda, and I get the feeling he's more sensitive than the average guy, because he admits he enjoys watching reality shows with his girlfriend and her friends. He told me how sorry he was and if I ever needed to talk he was there and if I wanted to come to a Bible study with him sometime I was always welcome.

The whole team knows why I'm a year late to accept the scholarship. I don't mind that people don't bring it up. It's not a subject conducive to locker room talk. But I appreciate Todd's giving me an outlet if I need it. I hope I won't.

The girls on campus have been especially attentive to my needs. I'm the shiny new fresh meat, and they're not shy about hinting they'd like a taste. One girl in particular, Amber McCa-

phrey, a sophomore volleyball player, has made herself particu-
larly available. She took it upon herself to pay me a personal visit
when I moved in, and volunteered her time as my private welcome committee. She showed me around campus, gave me a tour
of the library, and her house, and even her bedroom. Ideally, that's
where every great tour ends, right? But my mind's too occupied to
think about her, and my heart's too full to make space for her. She
only magnifies what I miss about Dylan, and instead of making
me forget, she makes it harder to move on.

The guys on the team think I'm crazy to pass her up. Amber's
got legs that keep going. Typical volleyball player body — long
and lean and an ass that's made for spandex, or maybe it's the
other way around. But she knows it. And she knows how to use
this arsenal of sexual energy to get what she wants. She wears the
miniskirts to prove it. And her hair and her face are always done
up, even when she's working out.

She also plays the leaning game. Very well.

But she tries too hard. She notices her appearance in anything
she passes that offers a reflection. She smells like a box of perfume.
Nothing is ever out of place. And to most people she's perfect. But
to me it's so far from it, because my idea of perfect is being too
busy laughing at yourself to care what you look like.

I don't go more than an hour without wondering where Dylan
is and who gets to hear her stories and make her laugh, and I have
to shove the thoughts out of my head before I want to shred something.

* * * * *

*After a month has passed, I decide it's time to call her.* It occurs to
me that I've still never talked to Dylan on the phone. We've fallen
in love and had sex and told each other our life stories, but we've

never even called each other. This is so backwards.

I made her give me her home phone number in Wisconsin before she left. She tried to convince me that we shouldn't try to get ahold of each other. We should leave it in fate's hands. Well, she can be the daydreaming optimist, but I'm going to be the levelheaded realist and know fate can only get you so far. It can put you down the right path or introduce you to a particular person, but the rest is up to you. Even the strongest storms need a wind to carry them in.

I pick up the white card her number and address are scribbled on and tap it on my nightstand. I sit on my bed and lean against the wall and dial the ten digits that will connect me with somebody that still holds the world in her hands.

It rings four times, and I'm about to hang up, and then a woman answers, sounding out of breath. I know it isn't Dylan, because she sounds older.

"Hi, I'm a friend of Dylan's?" I say it like it's a question because *friend* isn't quite the word I'd choose, but *lover* or *sexual partner* probably wouldn't be appropriate. We never tried to label what we had.

"Oh," she says. "You must be Gray." Bam. Nails it on the first try. I can see where Dylan gets her intuitiveness from.

"Yeah," I say, and hesitate, because I hadn't planned this out. I don't want to sound all needy and ask where Dylan is and who she's with and if she's talked about me and if she misses me and all the things I'd pay to know.

"I'm Dylan's mom," she says, all light and easy. "I was wondering when you'd call. It's been, what, a month now?"

It's been a month and six days since the morning she left. Way too long, in my opinion. But who's keeping count?

"Yeah," I say.

"I've heard so much about you," she says, and she tells me she

feels like she knows me. I rest my elbow on my knee and I'm starting to relax. Then I hear her scream, "Serena, Dylan's boyfriend
is on the phone," and my stomach cramps at the word *boyfriend*
because even Dylan's never called me that, and then I hear the
other line pick up and this younger girl gets on the phone.

"Is this Gray?" she asks, and I say yes and she screams and
tells me she knows we had sex, and then she hangs up.

I can feel blood flowing to my face. I pull the phone away, drop
my head, and mumble, "Oh, my God." Could this be going any
worse? I can hear Dylan's mom saying something, and I reluctantly put the phone back to my ear.

"Oh, Gray," she says, all consolingly, and she apologizes and
says Serena is sixteen going on six. She tells me not to be embarrassed, because if Dylan loves me I'm family now, so we might as
well open up.

Like that helps.

Then she actually keeps talking about it. So much for a light,
easy conversation. She tells me Dylan must be head over heels in
love with me to want to have sex, because she's always been a little
cautious in that department. The only boy she thinks Dylan has
ever kissed besides me was her neighbor, Spud Seebly.

"And he was a nice boy, but he had braces and his name was
Spud, so let's face it: how good could he be?"

"Um," I say. I am beyond desperate to get the topic off my sex
life with her daughter. And, really, Spud Seebly? What kind of
parents willingly name their kid Spud? They should be arrested
for douchebaggery.

"Dylan isn't around, is she?" I ask.

I get this highly amused laugh for an answer. She starts rambling again, it must be a family trait, and tells me Dylan was barely home long enough to shower and eat and she acted more excited
to see the dogs than her own family.

Sounds like Dylan.

"I swear, she's part bird, Gray. She was out of that damn bridesmaid's dress, which she looked beautiful in, by the way, and into that sorry excuse for a car of hers before I could say hello."

I run my finger along the headboard of my bed and stare out the window. The sun is setting behind the rooftops and my eyes travel as far west into the horizon as I can see. I ask her if Dylan's in California yet. Another small laugh answers me.

"Your guess is as good as mine. Last I heard she was in Boise, staying with her cousin for a few days. To earn spending money, they were going to help some firefighters build a trail. Don't ask me how she finds these random jobs."

I try not to get jealous at the image of strapping firefighters spending quality time with Dylan.

We talk a little bit more about the summer, and then Dylan's mom asks me all these questions about school, way more than my own mom asks. I ask her when Dylan plans on moving to Shasta City to start her job. She can't roam around carefree forever. Or, maybe I don't want her to be free. Maybe I selfishly want her to be tied down so I always know where to find her.

"I think she starts next week," her mom says. She tells me her aunt paid her way too much to sit around her pool this summer, snapping pictures.

"She did some painting," I say in Dylan's defense.

"Painting, that's a nice story. Aunt Dan gave that girl money just to sleep in a king-size bed and entertain her housekeeper. Two thousand dollars for doing nothing. That's no way to teach Dylan any kind of work ethic. That girl needs to learn charm will only get you so far in life."

Two grand is pretty generous. Dylan never told me how much her aunt gave her.

"That should last her for a while," I say.

I can hear her shaking her head. "One would think. But Dylan gave most of it to the animal shelter when she got back. Money runs through that girl's fingers like sand." She asks me to hang on for a second and then comes back to the phone and tells me she has to go, dinner is burning, but it was great to talk.

"Call back anytime," she says.

I panic.

"Wait," I say. "Can you give Dylan my number the next time she calls?" Her mom says yes, of course, and I give her both my cell and home number. She reads each number back to me to make sure she got them right.

"Tell her I'd like to hear from her."

"Oh, Gray, we'd all like to hear from Dylan. Who wouldn't?"

When I hang up my head is in the clouds, because for a brief moment I was back in Dylan's life, soaring along with her. But then I come down to the white walls of my bedroom and the state of New Mexico, and I'm excited to be here. But sometimes I have to remind myself to be excited because I wonder if I'd be happier just following her. I wonder if it's okay to let a single person be the center of your life.

## Dylan

*I'm sitting in a dusty parking lot* in Northern California, in the complete unknown, which oddly makes me feel complete. I love this vagabond lifestyle, this feeling of weightlessness. I couldn't be happier because I'm free. I've set off on another journey to discover places and people and fill up the holes of wonder inside me that grow wider and deeper the longer I stay in one place. I want to empty the basin of all that's known and predictable and fill my life with new experiences, with rainbow liquids that change colors with the touch of a finger. I want to create my own world by stepping out of the places I know.

I sit on the curb next to my car and drink gas station coffee (it only tastes good when you're on the road). This rugged scenery suits me. People told me to move to San Francisco or check out Carmel, or the wine country. But I don't want a polished atmosphere. I'm more intrigued by these high desert plains, these scrubby bushes and scraggly trees, barely clinging to life. The people here are rough cut too, as if everybody's working overtime to survive. In the distance Mount Shasta pierces through the clouds and spreads out before me like nature's giant welcome sign. My new home. The peak towers 14,000 feet in the sky and has been described as "lonely as God and white as a winter moon." The mountain looks misplaced, standing all alone with its head in the clouds. I feel like we have that in common.

I met a man yesterday, in Weed, California, who owns a brewery. He told me you only go around this world once. You've got to make the most of it. So, every day, with everyone I meet and everywhere I go, that's what I'll set out to do. If you wake up every day determined to make the most of it, how can you ever be disappointed?

Today I met a woman who owns a bakery in Yreka, California, an old gold mining town close to the border of Oregon. The steep hills around it are dusted with metal and gleam in the sun, teasing people to believe there's a treasure buried inside. It's the kind of a town where the local hardware store doubles as a coffee shop and cowboys pull up around a horseshoe-shaped counter to drink coffee next to shelves of fishing tackle.

Next door to the hardware store is a bakery, where I ordered the best cinnamon roll I've ever tasted — so sweet, the sugar danced in my mouth. When I asked Lila, the owner, what the secret ingredient was, she told me it was happiness. She said when you put happiness into what you cook, it tastes so much better. She told me when you put happiness into your job and your relationships, they grow. If you're not enjoying what you're doing or who you're doing it with, it won't turn out, she told me.

I want my life to be like that. I want it to be mouthwatering, savory, and memorable with every bite. It's strange how people tell you things at the exact moment you need to hear them. Words can be the most comforting of all. They can pick you up and keep you moving.

But no matter how much I gain, there is something even greater I lack, because one memory keeps chasing me.

I can't go an hour without thinking about Gray.

You know you love someone when he makes all the ordinary moments feel extraordinary. When doing absolutely nothing feels like everything. Gray assumed he wasn't enough. And what I didn't admit, what I didn't realize at the time, is that it's just the opposite. He was too much. That kind of love is the kind that traps you. And I'm not ready for it yet.

That's why I need to leave him alone. Distance is the best thing.

I stare out at the horizon and wonder what it would be like if you could have two lives, side by side. Your self and your alter ego. One life would be safe, predictable, and accepted. You'd follow the social guidelines: college, marriage, kids, career, golden retriever, and a two-story home in the suburbs. But I think everybody has this inner spirit, this dream of where their potential could take them if they were willing to break out of the norm and take risks. Most people hold their fantasies out of reach, as if their desires are a mountain they could never summit. They settle for living at the base of the mountain instead. There aren't as many obstacles, or avalanches, or unexpected delays. But they'll never be able to see the view from the top.

I feel like I violently teeter between these two selves. And I've decided to chase my wild side. I don't want to have any regrets. I think the worst mistake in life is to wonder, *What if?* I'd rather fail miserably pursuing my dreams than succeed at something I have to settle for.

I stand up and open my inspiration log to my page of *oughta*s. My goal for this week: *Let Him GO.* I stare down at the words with a frown. This goal is going to throw off my perfect record, because it seems impossible.

Why can't I block Gray out of my mind?

I know he has a million distractions. Moving. School. Baseball. Girls. That one really irritates me, but I try not to dwell on it, because we're all unique fingerprints. No matter who he meets, there's no one quite like me. People might be replaceable, but chemistry isn't. You can find other people to be attracted to, other people to crush on and laugh and hang out with. But you can't control who you click with. Who *gets* you—someone who can finish your thoughts, who shares your cells as though you have a molecular bond.

Deep down, I hope he's moved on. It's better that way. I hope, eventually, I will too.

# ‖‖ First Forget ‖‖

## Two Months Later

## Gray

*I try not to think about Dylan,* because when I do my brain flexes with anger. Was I that easy to forget? Was our summer together just a fling to her? Was I just a dwindling romance in her storybook life? Am I the one being a girl about all this? Because I thought what we had was real. I fricking proposed to this girl. And she can't so much as call me? She can't take two minutes out of her random day filled with God knows what and check in, tell me she misses me?

And that's the thought that hurts the most. She doesn't miss me.

And I miss her every day, especially at night. Nights give me the most trouble. I'm back to sleeping pills because I need something to numb my thoughts and turn off the stadium lights in my head.

The worst part is this internal battle that constantly plays out in my head, because underneath my anger and frustration (that's helping me throw really fast, by the way), I still love this girl. I want to be mad, I want to be furious, but then I look around at where I am and who I've become and I have her to thank for it. How can I be mad when I owe her so much?

I want to hear her voice. Hear her crazy thoughts. I want to live inside her brain for a day. Every day. I want to taste her. I want to lock her down. It's hard to stay mad at her when, really, all it comes down to is, I don't want to let her go.

✳ ✳ ✳ ✳ ✳

*Miles and I walk home from Lobo Field*, where we've spent a few hours in the batting cage. He has one of the purest swings I've ever seen, and he's been working with me on my form. My timing has always been off, and quitting for a year hasn't exactly helped my batting. I ask him if we can practice again tomorrow.

"Sure," he says. "I'll help you out, but only if you give me some advice."

We're walking with the sun on our faces, and I turn my baseball cap backwards so the rays can spill into my eyes. Two girls approach us on the sidewalk and they say hi to Miles and then they smile at me and I nod back. One of the girls follows me with her eyes and I can't help but notice her trip as she walks by. I hear them giggle and sprint away.

"What do you want to know?" I ask Miles. He's an outfielder with an amazing arm and the best hitter on the team. He only needs help narrowing down all the minor league teams interested in signing him.

"I want to know your secret with the ladies," he says, as if I should have guessed.

"What?" I stare at him.

"You draw them in like a fire, man. How do you do it?"

My eyebrows flatten with confusion. Miles is a great guy. I've heard girls say he's cute—he has dark red hair and brown eyes and more freckles than skin. He's always got a crooked grin on his face. He knows every person on campus by name. Everybody loves him. I'm cool just by association. And he thinks I'm . . . what? A ladies' man?

"Miles, what are you talking about?"

"I don't know, dude, but every girl asks about you." He admits it's getting annoying.

*"Who's Gray?"* he mimics in a high, feminine voice. *"He's so mysterious. He's so different from the other guys. He's so deep. Can he really play the guitar?"*

I shake my head and smirk.

"All I'm saying is, every girl wants to get in your pants," Miles says. "And it's a little frustrating. I always thought being an athlete was enough. Then you come around and mess up my only game. It sucks."

"That's not your only game, Miles," I say. "There's more to you than baseball." He just blinks back at me as though he's never considered this.

"You can't tell me you haven't noticed how girls fall all over themselves when you're around. It's like you can control them with your Jedi sex powers."

I laugh and tell him he's nuts. I tell him I just don't want to date right now and maybe girls are confusing it with my playing hard to get.

"What about Amber McCaphrey?" he asks, and he says her name like she's in the same league as Megan Fox.

I look back at him. "What about her? She's just a friend."

"Dude, she's every guy's number one draft pick for their fantasy spank bank team, and she's obsessed with you. Amber McCaphrey. Did you know she does swimsuit modeling?"

I smile. Modeling, huh? That would explain why her thoughts rarely extend beyond her body. Apparently food encourages not only fat cells, but thinking—two things models seem to be miss-ing, from my experience of knowing a few in high school. I decide not to share this observation with my new admirer.

"No," I say flatly. "I didn't know that."

His jaw drops at my indifference.

"You're not even impressed, are you?" Miles asks. I look over at him.

"Should I be?"

"Gray, she's the hottest woman I've ever seen in real life."

Suddenly a shocked expression fills his face and he stops walk-ing. I turn back and wait for him.

"Oh, shit. I get it. I finally figured you out."

I smile. "Oh, yeah?"

"Yeah." We keep walking, and he shakes his head with amaze-ment. "You don't even care. You're really above all that, aren't you? Looks don't even faze you. How many models have you been with?"

I throw up my shoulders up with a shrug. "Dude, I grew up in Phoenix."

"So?"

"Where did you grow up?" I ask.

He says on a farm in Mississippi.

"Exactly," I say. "You're just starstruck. See, every chick in Phoenix is hot and knows it, and runs around half naked all year round. You get desensitized."

"Never," he says, staring at me with jealousy, like I've been living in a taping of *Girls Gone Wild* for the last eighteen years.

"I'm serious," I say. "It's refreshing to meet someone who isn't all about her clothes and her image. It's nice to meet somebody who's real, who's beyond all the superficial crap. Who makes fun of it. You know?"

He shakes his head. "I have so much to learn," he says.

"You want to know one secret?" I offer.

He nods about seventeen times.

"I don't know much, but this is what I've learned. You'll fall for the last person you ever thought you'd be interested in. That's the tricky part. You might not even notice her at first. And she usually comes around just when you've stopped looking. But if you pay attention, you'll know it's her because she'll stand out from everybody else. She might even scare you. But if you're lucky enough to meet this girl, be smart enough to realize it and try not to screw it up," I tell him.

He's silent for a minute while he processes this.

"You're my new God," he says. "Will you please teach me?"

I just laugh and tell him sure, if he helps me work on my swing.

# ||| First Remember |||

## Gray

*My roommates decide to throw a party,* which is as simple as ordering a keg and having Bubba and Todd call their girlfriends. Three hours later our house is packed and Amber won't leave my side. I have a short taste of freedom when she goes to the bathroom, but then her friend and teammate, Melissa, backs me into a corner. She's an outside hitter and has some seriously defined biceps, so I'm a little intimidated, but I'm not going to let her see that. I stand as high as my six feet three inches will stretch, and meet her eyes.

"Stop messing with her head, Gray," she says, and she's drunk and rocking on her feet but glaring at me like she means serious business. "You mess with her, you mess with me," she says with attitude, as if I should watch my back, yo, or the women's volleyball team will be waiting for me in a dark, abandoned alley one of these nights.

I'm calm and keep my eyes steady on her not-so-steady ones. It was brought to my attention a few weeks ago that the volleyball team voted me as having the "best eyes" on campus, so I'm trying to use it to my advantage.

"I'm not messing with her head," I say. "I told her we're

friends. Friends," I repeat. "Want me to grab a dictionary and re-view that definition with you so there isn't any more confusion?" I grin and try to make light of it, but she scowls.

I'm determined not to let petty and catty girl qualms get to me. That's one thing I've learned after Amanda's death. When you experience a tragedy like that, it puts so much minor drama in perspective. I listen to my roommates freak out about dirty dishes or who drank whose milk or who left his wet laundry in the wash-er. I watch Todd sulk all day because he had one lousy practice, or Bubba get down on himself because he's too broke to take his girlfriend out for dinner one night. So many daily problems drift over my head. It's not that I'm above the drama—I just like to take a detour around it whenever possible. I know from experience things can turn so much worse.

Unfortunately, I'm learning this relaxed attitude only makes women more intrigued to *figure me out,* which honestly isn't in-tentional.

Melissa muffles a burp with the back of her hand. "Get over yourself, Gray. I see through your whole blue-eyed, nice-guy bullshit."

This makes me smile. I lift my baseball cap higher on my fore-head. "Really? What do you see?"

"You're a player through and through," she insists, and I just nod and tell her she's absolutely right, she's finally figured me out, and this makes her even more pissed.

"You know she likes you," she says, and jabs a finger hard against my sternum, and it actually hurts, but I try not to wince. "You're leading her on."

"I've never even touched her, Melissa. I've never asked her out. How is that leading her on?"

"Because Amber likes you," she repeats in this whiny drunk voice, which is really irritating. Why are girls determined to have emotionally heated conversations when they're drunk? In my observation, too much alcohol just makes guys one-dimensional hornballs and girls unpredictable basket cases, and under these dangerous circumstances they attempt to walk into the nearest house party and look for love. And people wonder why their relationships are so messed up.

I frown at Melissa. Now I'm going to get a shitty reputation because I'm trying to be a nice guy. I'm going to be a player and a tool just because I don't want to have sex with Amber McCaphrey. But if I do have sex with her I'll be a player and a tool for using her. I can't win.

I feel a tap on my shoulder and turn around and Amber's standing there ready to hit me with Operation Confront Gray: Phase 2. She has a cell phone in one hand and a red plastic cup in the other. She flips her ponytail over her shoulder.

"What are you and Mel talking about?" she asks with these curious, innocent blue eyes even though it is obvious she planted this entire conversation. I know how girls work. It was a premeditated attack planned twenty minutes ago next to the beer keg.

It's time to be blunt with this girl, because being friendly is making me too big of a jerk, evidently.

"Amber—"

And Miles interrupts me.

"Gray, the phone's for you," he yells over the music. Amber pulls on my arm.

"We need to talk, now," she informs me. I sigh and turn back to Miles.

"Who is it?"

He shrugs. "Some lady," he yells.

I frown because I forgot we had a land line. We only signed up for one to get a better cable deal. Must be my mom.

"Tell her I'll call her back," I say, and look down at Amber, who's drawing circles on the sleeve of my shirt with her index finger.

I want to be honest and tell her I don't like her, and maybe I would, but she ruins it because she tries too hard to impress me and it's all an act. Why can't she just be real? She stares into my eyes with that lovesick gaze, but it just makes me miss Dylan, the one girl who never looked at me that way. Every sentence Amber says begins with "I." That's the complete opposite of Dylan, and the more girls I meet, the more I'm realizing what a gem I discovered back in Phoenix.

Amber has a few other strikes against her. Not to be picky, but she refuses to play video games. She thinks Ms. Pac-Man's pointless. Pointless? Ms. Pac-Man is a metaphor for life. And Amber hates Bob Dylan. She thinks his voice is too whiny and nasally. Has she even listened to his poetic genius? Bob Dylan is more than human. He's a religious experience.

One time I let Amanda's name slip into the conversation when I was talking to Amber. I wanted to test her to see how she'd react. She cringed and got so uncomfortable with the topic, you'd think I'd just pointed out a huge zit on her forehead or asked her what her calorie intake was up to that day. That's when she lost my respect.

It's not that I'm better than Amber. Far from it. The problem is, I already know someone exists out there who is so much better for me.

I set my hands lightly on her shoulders. "Amber, listen—"

"Gray!"

I suck in a deep breath and turn to Miles.

"What?"

He walks right up to me and throws an arm around my shoulder. He's holding the phone in his hand. He's drunk and leaning in to me and he's shouting, even though his mouth is three inches away from my ear.

"Dude, this girl's talking crazy! I asked her who she was and she made me try to guess and when I couldn't guess she told me she was part mermaid, part water nymph and I'm really freaking out right now."

"What?" This is definitely not my mom. And it hits me. I grab the phone out of his hand. My heart's pounding. I look at Amber and she's seething.

"We'll talk," I say. "Just give me a few minutes."

"You're such an asshole," she yells, and tries to slap me as I turn away. I duck under a blow from her hand and run up the stairs, my adrenaline soaring at the thought of who I finally have in my grasp. I hurry into my bedroom and shut the door. I head to the fire escape and step out into the cool fall air. A light mist is falling, and it feels like a christening. I press the phone to my ear.

"Hello?" I say. And it's her.

# Dylan

*My heart speeds up at the sound of his voice.* It makes all the memories flood back. I'm still doubting if I should have called. It's a sweet temptation to open up the past, but then you invite it back into the future.

"Hey, you," I say.

"Dylan?" he asks, even though he knows it's me. It's like he just wants to say my name out loud.

"You might need to counsel your roommate. I think I scared him a little."

"Most women do," he says.

"I'm interrupting a party," I say.

"You're not interrupting anything," he says, and gets right to the point. "What took you so long to call?"

I freeze up. I hadn't expected this question so fast. No small talk?

"I thought maybe first we could break the ice by talking about the weather in our respective locations, or maybe roller derby and whether or not it should be inducted into the Olympics."

I hear an annoyed breath stream through the phone. Okay, maybe not.

"I don't do small talk," he says, and I feel myself nodding. Of course he doesn't. That's one of my favorite things about Gray. Once you crack the thick surface, he's miles deep.

"Was it just a fling, Dylan?" he asks.

"You really want to get right to it."

"It wasn't a fling to me. This summer. It was the real thing. But I don't want to stretch this out anymore. So what's going on in your head?"

I hear the edge in his voice, a little anger and hurt. Mostly frustration. I know he's losing sleep again and I feel responsible, as if I started to teach him how to swim only to leave in the deep end too soon.

"I know," I say, and I don't know what I'm referring to because I can't remember what I said or what I need to say or why I called. It's all blending together, and too much time has passed. I thought this conversation would be easy. A quick recap of life's events. Just the highlights, not all the heavy details. I forgot that Gray prefers to dwell in the heavy details. And how am I supposed to translate what's in my head when I can't even decipher it myself? My mind is like one of those brainstorming webs, going in a hundred different directions until my thoughts are crawling off the page.

"Dylan?" Gray asks.

"I'm sorry," I say. "I honestly thought giving you some time would help. That's why I didn't call. I wanted you to get settled in first."

He knows what I'm getting at.

"You mean forget about you? Do you really think I'm that small-minded? Do you think after what we had, I'm going to move on just because you decide not to call?"

"I know," I say in this quiet, timid voice. Too quiet. I sink deeper into my chair.

"Maybe this wasn't the best way to start things off," he admits. "Maybe we should have started with small talk." I nod and my eyes start to water. I want to know what fills his days. Where he sleeps. What friends he made. But too many feelings press against my heart.

"So what happens now?" he asks.

"I honestly don't know," I say.

I hear him breathing into the phone and I imagine his face and those eyes. God, I miss those eyes.

"Well, I'll tell you what's going to happen," he says, and he take the reins, takes control of this while he has a chance. "I'm going to see you again, because it's not over between us." He tells me he has three weeks off over Christmas break and he's driving up to California to stay with me.

"It won't work," I say. I tell him I moved in with the owners of the coffee shop I work at, in an apartment above the store. They offered me housing in exchange for helping to babysit their two little kids on the weekends. "I'm sleeping in one of the kids' rooms because it's rent-free and I'm broke."

"Fine," he says. "I'll sleep in my car."

"Gray, I live in the mountains and it's freezing and you don't even own warm clothes," I say, for once sounding logical. Very uncharacteristic.

"Since when are you logical?" he argues. "Besides, I won't need clothes. You can crawl into my sleeping bag and keep me warm." A heavy sigh lifts my chest because he refuses to be discouraged. "Come to Phoenix," he tries. He tells me to stay with my aunt for the holidays. I chew on my bottom lip. I had thought about that before, but it just leads to another problem.

"And then what?" I ask.

"What do you mean?"

I ask him what happens after winter break, and he tells me we'll cross that bridge when we get to it.

"Long distance never works," I say.

I'm answered by complete silence and my stomach knots. We both know there's only one other alternative.

"So is this over?" he asks. I curl my fingers tight around the phone. I hate that I can't see him right now. It never occurred to me this might be my last conversation with Gray, that the point of this phone call wasn't to say hello but to say goodbye.

"Are we finished?" he asks.

"I don't want to do this over the phone," I say, and my voice starts to shake.

"Too bad."

Tears sting my eyes. They feel like they're on fire.

I tell him this is why I didn't want to call. I admit I thought he'd be distracted with school and friends and training and that his mind would slip off me.

"That's not how I work, Dylan. I'm not out of sight out of mind."

Tears spill from my eyes and run down my face. How could I forget this about him? I don't let myself get attached to people, but Gray does. That's why he hardly lets anyone in.

"Do you still love me?" he asks.

"I'll always love you," I say without hesitating. But Gray knows I love everyone and everything, and this doesn't comfort him.

"You have to end it," he says.

"I can't end it. I love you, Gray. I can't just end feeling that way because of distance. I'll always love you."

"Then say you want to see me again."

I tell him we can't force this. We need to believe that if we're meant to be together it will happen. I close my eyes and pray he doesn't think I'm insane.

"You're insane!" he shouts. "How will it *happen?*"

I tell him we just have to have faith that something will bring us back together, someday, when the timing is right. If we're meant to be, it will happen.

"So what do we do in the meantime?" he asks.

"We let each other go," I say. "We live our lives."

Gray yells that he can't just let me go because you don't give up on the people you love, but maybe I need to lose someone in order to understand that.

"You're dreaming," he says. "Call me when you decide to wake up."

He hangs up and I hold the phone limply in my hand. I slump down in my chair and my chest feels cold. Broken. Like something inside me was destroyed.

## Gray

*I need to destroy something.*

I storm back in my room and consider throwing that stupid poem she framed for me off my balcony. Then I notice the card with Dylan's number and address on it and I grab it. I'm careful not to look at it because I feel like my desperate mind will memorize the numbers, and I want to forget she exists. I rip it up into pieces and head into the bathroom connected to the back corner of my room and I flush them down the toilet. I slam the seat cover down and sit, because my legs are shaking.

What the fuck is she thinking? That fate's going to magically bring us back together? She really does live in a storybook. Doesn't she realize it takes effort? Even love takes work. It's not just a fucking fairy tale. All I know is when she's smart enough to realize this, it'll be too late. I'll be gone.

I take my hat off and throw it on the ground and pull my fingers through my hair and swear and kick the wall. I hate all the wasted hours and energy I spent missing her. Wanting her. More than anything, I hate that I believed she felt the same way — that I was just as hard for her to get over. I hear a pound on my bedroom door and I know who's standing behind it.

I pull myself up and open the door and Amber is standing there all pouty and mad, but she's also giving me those love-sick eyes. She still has a red cup in her hand. She waits for me to invite her in, and I move away from the door and she slides by, careful to rub her chest against my arm and her hip against my side as she passes. She sets the cup down on my dresser and turns to stare at me. I close the door behind me until I hear it click shut. My breaths are short and unsteady, and I'm trying to get a grip. She gazes at me in the dark room, lit only by a streetlight outside.

"You're an asshole," she says, but it's her weird way of flirting. I ask her why.

"Because you're playing hard to get," she says. "And I know you want me." I stare back at her and think this is the last thing I can handle. I'm barely hanging on right now. I cross the room toward her, and before I can say anything she reaches up and grabs my neck and pulls my mouth down to hers.

I tense up but then I close my eyes and tip my head down to taste her lips and I want her to drain my mind. I transfer all my anger into this kiss. Maybe it will dull the pain. I cup her face in my hands and press my mouth harder against hers, because I want to suffocate. She tastes like beer and cigarettes and she smells like a perfume advertisement. She reads my anger as passion and she slams her tongue deep into my mouth and drags her fingers down my back and I feel like we're starring in a soap opera because it's too forced and too choreographed. She's doing all these fancy moves with her tongue and her hands and she's moaning like she's getting off. But it isn't real.

She pushes me down on the bed.

She stands a few feet away and throws this seductive grin at me, but it leaves me cold. She slips her ponytail out of her hair and it falls long past her shoulders, and she flips it around so it covers half her face. I lie back on my bed, feeling like I'm having an out-of-body experience, like my mind is hovering somewhere in the corner of the room on the ceiling and I'm looking down at myself wondering what the hell I'm doing here. This beautiful girl is moving right in front of me, but it feels as intimate as watching a commercial.

I don't want to use Amber. I can't. It's not fair to her. I'm not looking for someone to fill my heart or my mind or my bed, because when you're lucky enough to know exactly who you want, then fuck the rehearsal. No one else will ever compare.

She peels her tank top off slowly and tosses it at me, and it hits me in the stomach and rests there and I don't move. I just watch.

She's going to strip for me?

The wood floor is thumping from the bass downstairs, and rap music filters in. Amber swings her hips and leans forward so I can get a good look at her cleavage and her black lacy bra, and then she slowly pulls a strap down over her shoulder and waits for me to smile or swoon or nail her because I'm so turned on.

But it has the opposite effect on me. I feel dirty, as if I'm cheating on Dylan. Dammit. I can't. I stand up and hand her the tank top. My hand's shaking.

"Amber," I say. "I'm sorry. We can't do this."

She stops swaying and stares at me.

"What?"

I don't say anything. I just hold the tank top in my hand and try to apologize with my eyes.

"Are you gay?" she asks. I shake my head, but I can't really blame her for wondering. What guy wouldn't have a hard-on right now?

"That phone call," I say. "That girl?" I trail off because I don't know how to describe what I'm feeling and who Dylan is to me. Sometimes words aren't enough.

She presses her lips together.

"That's your girlfriend, isn't it?"

I shake my head. "No," I say, because she's not. "But I'm still in love with her. I'm sorry." She just stares at me before grabbing her shirt and pulling it on with a huff. She slams my bedroom door in my face before I can explain. I grind my teeth together, then open the door and pound my feet down the stairs. I pass people making out on the staircase and Bubba offers me a manly high-five when he sees me coming down after Amber, but I ignore him. I shove my way through people dancing in our living room and walk out the front door and into the cool night.

I feel like a wuss and a freak and a jerk but more than anything foolishly in love with this girl who's just becoming another memory to me. It's raining out, and before I know it I'm blocks from the house and my hair's soaking wet and I'm wiping water out of my eyes. The street's empty and I laugh pathetically to myself because I feel like Led Zeppelin's song "Fool in the Rain" was written for this moment. But the rain doesn't do anything to quiet my thoughts or calm me down, so I keep walking, my anger chasing after me and my doubts keeping up the pace.

# ⫼⫼ First Surrender ⫼⫼

## *December*

## Gray

*I'm in my bedroom in Phoenix*, two days before Christmas, and it's eighty degrees outside. My windows are open because there's a decent breeze. I'm lying on my bed in some work-out shorts, listening to Cold War Kids and tapping my feet to the rhythm. I like their rock sound, but what I'd like even more is to fall asleep just once this month without pills.

I think maybe Cold War Kids is too hard and I decide the Eagles might be more soothing. Then I settle on Counting Crows.

And then I hear it. A knock on my bedroom window. I sit up and my pulse skips a beat, as if that knock was right against my heart. I think maybe I imagined it because my mind just wanted to hear it, but I get up anyway. I slip on a pair of sandals and walk outside. I stop when I see who it is.

Dylan's standing in my backyard. I blink and think I must be dreaming, but I swear it's real. She's just like I remembered. She's wearing her usual baggy jeans. Her hair's in a ratty ponytail. She's wearing some vintage-looking T-shirt promoting a city softball league.

"You didn't leave your back door unlocked," she tells me, as if I should have been expecting her.

I run my hands through my hair and try to form words into a sentence.

"What are you doing here?" I ask.

"I wanted to give you something," she says.

I notice she's holding this plastic bag and I ask what's in it and she says "Things" in this secretive voice. I ask her what kind of things.

"You might think it's dumb," she says.

I rest my hands on my hips. "Dylan, we never would have made it past day one if I thought any of your ideas was dumb."

"You have a point," she says.

She explains every day we've been apart she's collected stuff that reminds her of me. She collected one thing a day. She says the bag's full of letters she wrote, rocks she found, photographs and postcards. She admits she has a new habit of asking people what their favorite quote is, so a lot of it is written-down quotes that she thinks I'd appreciate.

"It's probably a hundred things. That's about how many days it's been seen I've seen you."

I look down at the bag and tell her I'm impressed she kept it to one.

"Oh, there are four more in the car. It's my Christmas present to you."

I blink at her, and even though I shouldn't be surprised, I always am.

"Great," I say. "Maybe by next Christmas I'll be finished opening them."

I ask her if she drove Pickle all the way down here, and her mouth sinks into a frown.

"Pickle died a few weeks ago," she says, and I honestly feel bad hearing it. I fell in love with her in that piece of crap car. She says now she drives this green Buick she named Big Blue, and I don't bother asking her how she picked that name. She says he's okay but he thinks he's a professional ice skater because sometimes he likes to slide through stop signs or intersections when she'd prefer it if he just came to a complete stop.

"He's a showoff," she says, and I'm grinning and it feels like no time has passed, just minutes. Maybe seconds. We're both quiet for a moment, and I ask Dylan if she likes living in California. I want her to say she hates it and she's moving to New Mexico. I want her to say she's miserable without me, but I don't think Dylan's capable of being miserable.

"I like anywhere I go," she says. "Every place has something to offer."

This is a little too optimistic.

"So, you're saying if you had to live in Siberia, you'd like it?"

"Sure," she says. "I've always wanted to dogsled. I'd build a log home and hunt for my food and make clothes out of animal fur and I'd use the teeth and bones to make necklaces and jewelry and that's how I'd earn money."

I shake my head and sigh, because even though this sounds ridiculous, I can imagine her doing it.

"How are your parents?" she asks. It's always about other people. That's her number one concern. Others first, herself last.

I tell her they took a three-hour bike ride today and my mom's joined a book club and my dad's golfing again. They're doing better. Not great, but a vast improvement. I tell her my mom and I stayed up late last night playing Trivial Pursuit. I admit I hate that game more than anything but my mom loves it, and it was this monumental breakthrough to see her awake after nine p.m.

Dylan's eyes are dancing over me while I talk, and I ask her what she's looking at. She tells me I have more muscles now. And my stomach is flatter. I run my hand across my six-pack and tell her I sure as hell hope it's flatter, since I'm doing two hundred sit-ups a day.

She's staring at my stomach and then back at my eyes.

"You're tan," she points out.

"You're pale," I say, but her skin looks creamy and soft and I'm aching to touch it.

"Have you turned into one of those guys that flexes in front of the mirror?" she asks.

"I've always been one of those guys," I say, and she smiles.

"Are you going to get your ears pierced and wear diamond-studded earrings now that you're a big shot athlete?"

"Nah. Not until the Gatorade endorsement comes through," I say.

"Maybe you could look into doing g-string modeling in case the thing with Gatorade doesn't pan out."

I shake my head. "I'm not a huge fan of the g-string. It looks like butt floss."

She says that's too bad. I'd look great in leopard print.

I tell her I'll think about it, but not right now because I'm having a fat day.

She just stands there holding her plastic bag, and we're both quiet. She looks up at the moon for a few seconds, full and bright in the sky, and she asks me if I think it's a man or a woman's face inside it. When I don't answer, she tells me she thinks it's the face of a legendary alien named Vorth that united the galaxy six million years ago.

I ignore her freak creative outburst and ask her if she's having separation anxiety.

"Maybe a little," she admits. I mention there are all these

terrific forms of communication made easily accessible by advances in technology, like telephones and e-mail, that can help deter that.

"You're being snarky," she says.

"I haven't slept in a while." She nods because she knows I have a complicated relationship with sleep.

"Have you been thinking about Amanda?" she asks, and I tell her yeah, Amanda, and other girls that like to blow in and out of my life. I raise my eyebrows and wait for her to respond. It's time to get to the point. *Why are you really here?*

She sets the bag down on the ground and folds her fingers over each other as if she's about to pray, but I think she's just nervous.

I make Dylan nervous? I need to mark this day down on a calendar, because it's a first for me.

"I'm sorry I tried to stay away," she says. "At first I thought it would be easier for me, which it wasn't, and then I thought it would be easier for you, but I didn't get that impression during our little phone chat." She pauses and her eyes focus on mine. "I didn't call you last month to break up. I really want you in my life, Gray," she says.

I study her and think maybe I should still be bitter, but I can't be angry at Dylan. It would be such a waste of time. I'd much rather be kissing her. And she's here. She's making an effort. That's all the apology I need.

I tell her I'm sorry I hung up on her.

"All I wanted to do was avoid hurting you. That's it. I hated the idea of hurting you. And that's exactly what I did," she says.

I take a step toward her.

"I want to try to make this work," she says. "I don't want to have any regrets. And I'd regret not having you in my life."

My eyes rest on hers and I smile. My heart's hammering in my chest as if it's trying to push me to take another step forward.

"Anyway, you did invite me to come down here for the holidays. Does that offer still stand?"

I nod slowly. "I missed you," I say. "I thought about you every day. I just didn't collect things to prove it."

"Yeah," she says, and she scratches her chin while she con templates this. She tells me *miss* is such a vague word. It doesn't come close to defining how it really feels to crave someone.

"I guess *longing* might be better, or maybe *yearning*, but I hate that word. It sounds so whiny," she says. "I mean, who actually says, 'I *yearned* for you . . .'"

I listen to her ramble, something I missed, because her mind is like a kaleidoscope, always changing and rotating and impossible to predict. And I could rattle off how much I love her and try to express all the feelings that are rolling through my head, but I just grab her and pull her against me and kiss her like I've been dreaming about kissing her for the last three months.

I show her sometimes words can never be strong enough.

She kisses me back, and it starts out sweet and then turns into something else. She folds her arms around my neck. I pull her tight against me, and I can feel her heart pounding with mine, and everything else melts away.

I know I'll never be able to control what happens in my life or what people will slip in and out of it, the way time slips by and you can't get it back.

And I don't know for sure where I'm going to end up.

But I know who I love. And I'm figuring out that might be enough to live for.

# *Inspiration for* First Comes Love

This book started as a creative writing exercise I assigned to myself. For a Challenge, I decided to write a love story from the male perspective. What began as a couple of chapters quickly spilled out into an entire novel. I simply fell in love with my characters. I fell in love with their story.

I used to live in Phoenix, and while I was there I took classes at Mesa Community College, hiked many desert trails, learned how to play the guitar, took photographs with my old manual camera, and collected memories in my journal. There is no horizon as spellbinding as a desert sunset. It is a setting I couldn't wait to capture in a novel.

Although Arizona was a fascinating state to explore, with the most unique topography I've ever seen, I was miserable living in Phoenix. I hardly made any friends, so it became a long year of solitude and contemplation. It was easy to write Gray's character, because in many ways I was brooding and annoyed, just the way he started out. I couldn't stand the showy scene in Phoenix or the people or the constant heat. But in a lot of ways I was like Dylan, trying to soak up every experience and never waste a single moment. Phoenix is just one of the many pit stops I took while I was living like a vagabond for about four years. In a lot of ways I was Dylan, always on the lookout for a Gray—someone to share my ridiculous adventures with—and in many ways I was Gray looking for a Dylan—someone refreshing to dig me out of the depressing state I was sinking into, dust me off, and make me laugh.

The other part of this story, Gray's struggle to deal with his sister's death, is inspired by an amazing friend I made in Oregon. Her brother and best friend had recently passed away when we met, and she was slowly attempting to pick herself up and move forward. Her way of grieving was to talk about her brother, and she kept his memory alive by sharing stories. I felt as if I knew him even though I never had the privilege of meeting him. I even spent a day with her honoring her brother (on the anniversary of his death). We wore his photograph around our necks, we looked at pictures while she told me stories, we listened to music he loved, and this experience inspired the scene that Gray and Dylan share together.

I owe so many of my stories to the places I travel and the brilliant, hilarious people I'm fortunate to meet. Some of the scenes in this book really happened. I ran down Mulholland Drive once, with one of my best friends, while cars careened past us. We sang Bob Dylan songs and raced all the way to Hollywood Boulevard. (I've also driven down Mulholland plenty of times, and I recommend it to running.) I've hiked all over Sedona (one of my favorite places in the world) and sat for hours in mediation spots. And if you ever want to take some stunning pictures of saguaro cactus, definitely check out Picacho Peak State Park, outside of Phoenix. I went there several times to take pictures by myself.

This book is half dream and half reality, half experiences I've had and half experiences I would love to have. I guess that's why I love writing. I get to live out my dreams for a while.

# *Playlists*

While I wrote, I compiled playlists that helped me build Gray's and Dylan's characters. Just for fun, I'm also including one of the mixes Gray made for Dylan.

GRAY:

1. MY LIE  *The White Buffalo*
2. THIS IS SUCH A PITY  *Weezer*
3. MYSTERIOUS WAYS  *U2*
4. TO BE YOUNG  *Ryan Adams*
5. JOY RIDE  *The Killers*
6. NEARLY BELOVED  *The Wallflowers*
7. I WANT YOU  *Bob Dylan*
8. ROCK AND ROLL  *Eric Hutchinson*
9. JUST LIKE HEAVEN  *The Cure*
10. JULY, JULY  *The Decemberists*
11. NEVER HAD NOBODY LIKE YOU  *M. Ward*
12. WHATEVER YOU LIKE  *T.I.*
13. TEAR IT OFF  *Method Man and Redman*
14. FOOL IN THE RAIN  *Led Zeppelin*
15. HANG ME UP TO DRY  *Cold War Kids*
16. ELEVATION  *U2*


DYLAN:

1. KODACHROME  *Paul Simon*
2. OPTIMISTIC THOUGHTS  *Blues Traveler*
3. I DON'T KNOW WHY  *Alison Krauss*
4. WHEN YOU FEEL IT  *Brett Dennen*

5. FIVE YEARS TIME  *Noah and the Whale*

6. SWEETEST THING  *U2*

7. ALL SUMMER LONG  *Phoebe Kreutz*

8. RAIN KING  *Counting Crows*

9. RUDIE CAN'T FAIL  *The Clash*

10. THE UNDERDOG  *Spoon*

11. IF YOU WANT SING OUT, SING OUT  *Cat Stevens*

12. I HEAR THE BELLS  *Mike Doughty*

13. THE LITTLEST BIRDS  *The Be Good Tanyas*

14. SAY HEY  *Michael Franti*

15. LIVE YOUR LIFE  *T.I.*

16. TRUE OR FALSE  *Bishop Allen*


GRAY'S MIX TO DYLAN:

1. CALIFORNIA  *Joey Ryan*

2. FRESH FEELING  *The Eels*

3. LOVER  *Devendra Banhart*

4. DON'T BE SHY  *Cat Stevens*

5. THE BOOK OF LOVE  *The Magnetic Fields*

6. YELLOW  *Coldplay*

7. LET'S GET IT ON  *Jack Black*

8. ROMEO AND JULIET  *The Killers*

9. IT'S LOVE  *Chris Knox*

10. CRAZY LOVE  *Adam Sandler*

11. I'LL KEEP IT WITH MINE  *Bob Dylan*

12. BURNING LOVE  *Elvis Presley*

13. HAWKMOON 269  *U2*

14. HALLELUJAH  *Jeff Buckley*

15. PEACEFUL EASY FEELING  *The Eagles*

# Acknowledgments

Thanks to Helen Breitwieser for being my agent, my sounding board, and sometimes my therapist. Thanks to Julia Richardson, my editor, for helping to shape this book into its best form. Thanks to Houghton Mifflin Harcourt for taking on this book and believing it was special. Thanks to Ryan (with whom I've actually run down Mulholland Drive) for making me fall in love with Bob Dylan—although my love will never surpass yours. Thanks to Gail, my grandmother, for always encouraging the wild and adventurous Dylan inside of me, and to my parents for all of their love and support. Thanks to the town of Sedona for, well, existing. Thanks to some of my hilarious, strong, and creative friends, such as Jill Weidenbaum, Karin Morris, Becky Bechtell, Marcia Doran, and Val Peck, who have inspired as well as participated in some of my greatest moments. Thanks to Mark Thompson, my guitar teacher in Phoenix. Thanks to my sister for your recommendations on my three greatest passions: books, movies, and music. Thanks to Kelley Croco for your feedback on my rewrites. Thanks to the Wisconsin Woodchucks for making me fall in love with baseball (and making my summer nights much more memorable), and, always, a huge thanks to Adam for being so consistently wonderful.